# With Friends Like These, Who Needs Enemies?

D0802947

# With Friends Like These, Who Needs Enemies?

Angela Shelf Medearis
Illustrated by Robert Papp

SCHOLASTIC INC.

New York   Toronto   London   Auckland   Sydney
Mexico City   New Delhi   Hong Kong   Buenos Aires

*To my childhood friends, JoAnne Wall Silva and*
*Barbara White Melin, with love*
*— Angela Shelf Medearis*

Cover design by Janet Kusmierski.

Text copyright © 2003 by Angela Shelf Medearis.
Illustrations copyright © 2003 by Robert Papp.
All rights reserved. Published by Scholastic Inc.
Printed in the U.S.A.

ISBN 0-439-12413-1
(meets NASTA specifications)

3   4   5   6   7   8   9   10          23          13  12  11  10  09  08  07  06

# Contents

# Chapter One

## Field Day

The Joyland Scream-a-rama roller coaster spun out of control. The cars careened around the curves at breakneck speed. I clenched the bar as our car's seat harness cracked, snapped, and then popped open. The car seat swung wildly back and forth. Sandra lurched forward and almost fell out of the seat. I grabbed her just in time. She squeezed my arm tightly.

I could see the attendant down below wrestling the lever to stop the giant roller coaster. Sandra's screams pierced the air, cracking one of my glasses' lenses.

"Hang on, Sandra," I said as I squeezed her arm and tried to hold her inside the car.

Sandra kept screaming something over and over.

The wind was rushing past and I couldn't hear her. I felt like I was dreaming.

"What did you say?" I shouted.

"You are the most beautiful, wonderful sister any girl could have." Then she hit my shoulder and shook my arm again.

I frowned. "What kind of way is that to thank me?" I said. "And why are you hitting my shoulder? That hurts."

"Wake up, Sharie," Sandra said, hitting my shoulder again, harder this time. She switched on the light.

I realized I was squeezing my pillow, not saving Sandra's life. It was all just a dream. I pushed the pillow away and pulled the covers over my head.

"Leave me alone! I just saved your life."

In reality, my thirteen-year-old sister, Sandra, didn't ride the Scream-a-rama at Joyland. Annette, my best friend, and I rode it together once. It was my big idea to ride it. I had bugged my mother all summer to get permission. When I finally got on the Scream-a-rama, it scared me to death. I actually passed out after the ride. Thank goodness Annette has never told anyone about the Scream-a-rama ride. That's the kind of friend she is.

I yawned, rolled over, and tried to go back to sleep. In my dream, I wasn't afraid to ride the Scream-a-rama.

"Okay. Lay there, goofybrain," Sandra said, switching off the light.

"Next time, I won't save you," I mumbled. But she had already huffed out of the room.

I peeped out from under the covers. The clock light shone brightly — it was 4 A.M.! Oh, no. Not again! I groaned.

The other big thing that happened this summer is that my father came home from the navy. The bad part about it is that he still operates on navy time. And he makes *us* live like *we're* all on navy time, too.

Maybe if I pretend that I'm asleep, he'll forget about me. I snuggled under the covers, turned my back to the door, and squeezed my eyes shut.

I heard his footsteps. 1-2-3-4, 1-2-3-4. Oh, no.

"All hands on deck!" Daddy said. "Hop in the head — I mean, the bathroom — wash up, and we'll rendezvous in the galley at 0430 hours."

It amazes me how things can change so much in such a short time. When Daddy shipped out for his last navy tour, I was eight years old. Daddy was like my best buddy. But now I'm ten, and to be honest, he's driving me nuts.

Daddy gets up every single morning before the sun and tears around the house — slamming doors, running the vacuum cleaner, and clanking pots and pans in the kitchen. The first week I thought it was great that Daddy helps Momma while she's at work. But he was having a hard time adjusting to being off the ship — last week he woke us up at 0430 hours to have a "field day."

At first, I didn't know what he meant. So I said, "Great, a field day!"

Sandra's older, so she knew better. She grumbled all the way into the galley — that's what Daddy calls the kitchen.

Daddy forgets he's not on the ship, so at any moment you might need to whip out a dictionary of navy terms. The alarm clock in my parents' room doesn't even ring anymore, it plays reveille.

"Sharie, get up now," Daddy said sternly. He was standing in my doorway. He clicked the lights on and off.

I hate for him to fuss at me, so I groaned and pulled the covers over my head. To be honest, I don't like anyone telling me what to do. That's what I hate about being a kid. Everyone thinks they have the right to tell you what to do. But I can't tell anyone what to do.

If I had a pet, I could tell the pet what to do. Only my parents won't let me have a pet. Daddy says we move around too much to worry about uprooting a pet.

Daddy yanked the covers off the bed. "Up now, sailor! March to the galley immediately!"

He tickled my feet and left the room. I couldn't help but giggle. Then I stumbled into the bathroom to get ready for breakfast.

Every Saturday morning, Daddy prepares what he calls "the big breakfast." That means a huge mound of fluffy scrambled eggs, half a package of crisp bacon, a stack of buttered toast, a pitcher of fruit juice, and a big bowl of hot cereal. Daddy's plate of eggs

5

and bacon is floating in a sea of hot sauce. He puts it on everything he eats.

"Daddy, I keep telling you that I don't eat meat anymore," Sandra said as she pushed the bacon to the side of her plate.

Here we go. The two of them are at it again. I don't feel up to hearing Daddy lecture this time of morning, so I say, "Daddy, is our field day like last Saturday? Running, hiking, and exercising until we drop dead from exhaustion?"

"No sir, crew members," Daddy said as he speared Sandra's bacon with his fork. "Since your mother has to work on Saturdays, I developed a list of household duties. The items that have a trouble call number beside them are for me. The rest of the cleaning is split between the two of you. We need to time our work around PCS moves so that we'll be ready for a zone inspection when your momma gets home."

"Huh?" I said, staring at him. "What does that mean? What are PCS moves?" I didn't really want to know what he meant. PCS moves sounded like a lot of work.

"Thank goodness," Sandra piped in. "PCS moves mean that we have to work until we drop dead from exhaustion."

Daddy said, "Hard work never killed anybody. The navy teaches you to . . ."

We both jumped up to clear the table. Daddy can talk about the navy for hours.

"We'll get started on our chores now," Sandra said.

"Great!" Daddy said. "We have a lot of work to do."

Sandra and I gave each other a look behind Daddy's back. Every now and then we are on the same wavelength. It doesn't happen often, but when it does, it works. Anything was better than hearing Daddy lecture about the navy, even if it meant cleaning up all day on a Saturday, starting before the sun came up.

# Chapter Two

Not Again!

I slept almost all day on Sunday. I was exhausted from the "wonderful field day we had." At least, that was the report Daddy gave Momma. I must admit, she was pretty happy to see the house sparkling clean from top to bottom.

Momma cooked a big Sunday dinner. Then we all sat around and watched a movie. It was fun to be together again. I'd missed having Daddy around. Maybe after a few more weeks he'll get the navy out of his system and we can start sleeping late on Saturdays again.

On Monday, as soon as I got off the bus, I burst through the door to tell Momma that I made the Step

Team. The Step Team cheers and performs during the after-school basketball and football games.

I tried out when I was nine, but I wasn't chosen. Sandra was on the Step Team when she was nine, but of course, she does everything perfectly. Sandra plays the piano, makes good grades, fixes her hair all by herself, and on and on and on. It isn't right for one person to have so many talents. Finally, I can say that I made the Step Team, too!

I raced into the kitchen, but Momma wasn't there, even though I smelled food cooking. Daddy had gone to the naval base for the day. Momma said she was taking the day off to rest.

I was glad she was home today because I couldn't wait to tell her about the Step Team. But where was she? The door to her room was closed. I knocked.

"Come in," she said, almost whispering. I hesitated. What if somebody had broken in and was holding her captive? What if she was signaling for me to run and get the police by whispering? What if . . .

"Sharie, what are you doing out there?" Momma said. "Come on in."

I opened the door. Momma was sitting on the bed, holding the phone. So that's why she was whispering. She signaled for me to sit.

I sat down on the bed beside her. I could see that she'd been crying.

"What's the matter?" I said.

"Shhhh," she said, holding her finger up to her mouth.

"No problem, honey. Of course, I'm glad. We'll talk about it some more when you come home."

It was Daddy. They always used a special tone of voice with each other. Momma never yelled at Daddy and he never yelled at her. What did he say that would make Momma cry?

Momma hung up the phone, wiping her eyes with the back of her hand.

"What's the matter?" I asked her, trying not to blurt out my good news until I knew what was wrong.

"I'll tell you when Sandra gets here. No need to repeat myself."

"I'll repeat it for you, Momma. Tell me, tell me,

please, tell me," I begged. "Miss Prissy Sandra might not be coming straight home. Sandra might be . . ."

"Why are you talking about me again?" Sandra said, popping into the room. She hugged Momma.

"What happened, Momma? Are you sick? Do you want to lay down and rest?"

"No, thanks. Sit down, both of you," Momma said.

"I'm already sitting down," I said.

Momma sighed loudly. "I can see that, Sharie. You always have to have the last word, don't you?"

Why did I say that? I have the biggest mouth!

"I have some good news to tell you," Momma said, smiling.

I wanted to ask, If it's such good news, why are you crying? But I bit my lip before I could blurt it out.

"Your daddy just called. We're moving to Austin, Texas. And we're not going to be living on a military base. Isn't that wonderful?"

Just like that, my Step Team dreams were stomped into the ground. At first, I thought maybe Momma was just kidding. It can't be true. Daddy doesn't even like uprooting pets. Surely he's not taking us out of school after only three weeks. When we moved here two years ago, Daddy promised Momma it was the last move we'd make until he left the navy.

Momma explained that Daddy was leaving the navy and was taking a job at an airport in Austin, Texas. We were moving again. No, no, no! This couldn't be happening. Not again.

"I'm not going," I said. "You can do what you want, but I am not leaving my friends."

"Do you want to move, Momma?" Sandra said. "If it's okay with you, I think it's a good thing."

Now, why couldn't I have said that? Instead I heard words continuing to spurt out of my mouth. I couldn't seem to stop talking! I was also crying like a baby.

"It isn't fair," I said. "I just found out that I made the Step Team! What about my friends?"

"You mean *friend,* don't you?" Sandra said. "Annette's the only friend you have."

"Be quiet, Sandra. I'm not talking to you," I said.

"Don't talk to your sister like that, Sharie. I know

you're upset, but this is your daddy's chance to get a good job and a new house."

"What's wrong with this house?" I said. "I thought he loved the navy. What about all the lectures he makes us listen to about the navy? What about school? I don't know why I even bother to unpack! We're always moving!"

Momma started to cry again.

"See, now look what you've done," Sandra said. "You're upsetting Momma! Quit being so selfish!"

"I'm sorry, Momma," I said. But it was too late. She was really sobbing now and it was all my fault. Why do I talk before I stop to think? I should just keep my big mouth shut!

Momma was crying and Sandra was glaring at me. If I had a mirror, I'd glare at me, too. What on earth was wrong with me?

The next week, the movers came and took the furniture away. Momma took me to school so that she could transfer my records. I went to say good-bye to my new teacher, Miss Peters, and the kids in my class. I'd only been in school for a few weeks, so I didn't know anyone that well. It was hard, but I was proud of myself that I didn't cry.

Then I had to tell Mrs. Carter, the Step Team director, that I was moving. She hugged me and said that she would miss me. She said I did a great job during my audition and that I should keep dancing. I started to cry because I really wanted to be on the Step Team. I cried all the way home.

Saying good-bye to Annette was the hardest part of the day. She came over with her mother to say good-bye.

"I'll write to you, Annette," I said, tears streaming down my face.

"She won't be able to read your chicken scratch," Sandra whispered.

"Get lost," I yelled.

"Sharie, stop yelling," Momma said. "Can't you get along with your sister for one day?"

That's why I always say that Sandra is sneaky. She's always doing or saying something when Momma and Daddy aren't around. She whispers so low that no one can hear it but me.

"Make her leave me alone!" I whined.

"I didn't say a word, Momma," Sandra said.

She picked up a box to take to the car. She bumped into me when she passed by. I started to say something, but I decided to ignore her.

I gave Annette a big hug.

"I will never have another best friend as long as I breathe on the earth."

"Give us a break, Drama Queen," Sandra whispered.

"Momma," I said, "make Sandra move away from me."

Momma stormed over. "Say good-bye and let's get going. I'm too hot for this."

I hugged Annette again and got into the car. I waved good-bye as we pulled away from the curb. I could see the tears on Annette's face. I cried harder.

"Sharie, get a hold of yourself. You'd think we never moved before," Daddy said.

That was the problem. I was ten years old and we'd already moved eight times. Just when I was starting to have fun here, we have to move again.

I was looking for something to wipe my face with when I spotted something that distracted me. There was a letter stuffed into Sandra's coat pocket. I snatched it away.

"Give it back," she whispered. "Give it back right now."

I opened the letter and tried to read the scrawled writing. Sandra tried to grab the letter back, but Momma turned around and she pretended like she was fanning herself. I moved away from her and tried to read the letter. It said:

Dear Sandra,

    Roses are red
    Violets are blue
    Believe me girl
    I'm going to miss you.

Love always,
Robert Nichols

Sandra ripped the letter out of my hand, but I still had the bottom half of it. I stuck out my tongue at her and stuffed the piece of paper into my pocket.

"What are you girls doing?" Momma asked.

"I was just reading something," I said.

"What?"

Sandra looked at me, terrified that I was going to tell on her.

"Nothing special," I said.

Sandra breathed a sigh of relief. She mouthed the words "I'm going to get you." I just smiled.

I had something on my perfect older sister and she couldn't do anything about it. I took the torn half of the letter out of my pocket and whispered what was written there.

"P.S. Thanks, Sandra, for that sweet good-bye kiss." Sandra tried to snatch the paper out of my hand. I moved away from her and stuck it down my shirt. Sandra glared at me.

I sighed and leaned back with my hands folded behind my head. This wasn't going to be such a bad day after all. Every now and then during the long car ride,

I puckered up my lips and blew Sandra a kiss. She turned away from me and looked out the window.

The ride to Austin took forever. A car trip with Daddy is always an adventure. He might be out of the navy now, but he sure doesn't act like it. To him, we're still his shipmates. When we get something to eat, we stop for "chow." He calls the drinking fountain at the rest stop the "scuttlebutt." Who would want to drink out of something called a scuttlebutt? Not me. I was about to die of thirst by the time we got to Austin.

Our house was on a tree-lined street and was far back from the curb. The closest house was almost a half a block away. This was a first. Other than apartments, the only houses we'd ever lived in were on military bases. On most naval bases, all the houses were neatly sandwiched together.

Our new house was a big, rambling, light blue, wooden two-story. It had white trim around the windows. Momma started to cry the minute she saw it. I tried to be sensitive.

"Momma, don't cry. It's not so bad," I said, patting her on the back. "Maybe we won't have to stay here that long."

Daddy hugged her and frowned at me over her shoulder. Sandra just glared at me.

"I know that it's just a big, old house sitting out in the middle of nowhere," I continued. "But it could be a lot worse."

Momma stopped crying. She and Daddy both frowned at me.

"Why would you say a thing like that, Sharie?" Momma said.

"I don't know what's gotten into you," Daddy said. "You can be so ungrateful sometimes."

"But I . . ."

"But nothing," Momma said. "Apologize to your daddy. Howard, this house is lovely!"

I could see Sandra wanted to add her fifty cents, but she knew better.

"Momma, I thought you were crying because you didn't like it," I said.

"No, I'm crying because I love it. It's the first house we've ever owned."

"But I didn't think you liked it," I said.

"That's just it, Sharie," Momma said. "You speak before you think. You're getting too old to keep doing that! Now apologize so we can go in and see our beautiful new home."

"I'm sorry," I said, dropping my head. I never seemed to be able to say the right thing.

"Come on, shipmates, cheer up! You're going to love the overhead," Daddy said.

He meant the ceiling. Once we were inside I could see what he meant. The ceiling was so high even Daddy looked short, and he's 6'2".

Our furniture had already been delivered. I loved my room! It was huge. My old room was the size of a closet compared to this one.

Sandra's room was bigger than mine, of course. Momma said that was because she's the oldest. I don't think that's fair because I will never be the oldest. Does that mean I can never, ever have the biggest room? I didn't say anything to Momma. My big mouth had gotten me into enough trouble already.

# Chapter Three

Big Sister Blues

We were in a new place, but everything was still the same. Daddy started making all kinds of lists. Momma started sorting out things in the kitchen.

As soon as Momma and Daddy were busy downstairs, Sandra rushed into my room. She slammed the door shut.

"Give me back the rest of my letter," Sandra said.

"No way," I said.

I had already hidden the letter in a safe place. I knew Sandra would be looking for it the first chance she got.

"Promise you won't ever tell?" she said.

I frowned and waved my hand, my pinkie sticking out into the air as I spoke in a high-pitched voice like the actresses I'd seen on television.

"Really, darling. You can't expect me to make that kind of promise, can you?"

"Come on, please, Sharie," Sandra said. "If you give it back, I promise I'll stop picking on you."

I shook my head and clicked my tongue up against my teeth.

"Tsk, tsk, tsk," I said. "My dear sweet not-so-innocent-as-she-pretends-to-be Sandra. Even if I don't promise to keep your secret, I don't think you're going to pick on me anymore, now are you?"

"Why, you little weasel," she said, snatching my arm.

I brushed her hand away. "Get out of my room before I find that letter and show it to Momma."

"If you tell, I'll make your life miserable," she promised.

"Really? How will you do that after Momma reads that letter and grounds you for life?" I said. "Now please go."

Momma opened the door. "I hope you two aren't in here feuding again."

"No, ma'am. In fact," I said, still talking in my proper movie star voice, "Sandra just told me that I'm her very best friend. And she's going to let me have her white lace curtains for my room. Didn't you, Sandra?"

Sandra made a face that Momma couldn't see.

"Sandra! That's so nice of you," Momma said. "See, this house is making our lives better already. I think we're all going to love Austin!"

"Momma, I think you're right," I said with a smile. "I think I am going to love Austin, especially now that Sandra and I are best friends."

Momma gave me a big hug. I looked over her shoulder and saw Sandra sticking out her tongue at me. I can say one thing for the girl, she's willing to take chances.

"Come on over here, Sandra. Give us a hug," Momma said.

Sandra marched over like a robot. Momma put

her arms around the two of us. Sandra held the arm that would have hugged me down by her side.

"Don't be so stiff," Momma said. "Hug your sister better than that."

Sandra lifted her arm like she was a robot and hugged me stiffly.

"That's better," Momma said.

"Yeah, Sandra," I said. "That's better."

We spent all weekend unpacking boxes and putting things away. Sandra left me alone except when she threw the white lace curtains into my room. Momma helped me hang them up. They looked better with my bedspread than they did with Sandra's. I twirled around and around. I loved my new room!

Now that Daddy had a good job, Momma didn't have to work anymore. She was really happy to have a chance to stay at home. Sandra and I were happy because now we didn't have as many chores, even though this house was bigger than our old one.

Momma cooked something special every night. One night she prepared my favorite dinner, then Sandra's favorite vegetarian meal, then Daddy's, and then hers. I was glad she would be there every day when I came home from school.

I'm sure Sandra didn't like the fact that Momma would be home all the time. Sandra usually sneaks around while Momma is at work, doing stuff like talking on the phone, hanging around outside, or picking on me. Lately, Sandra has left me alone. She was using the silent treatment to bug me.

If Daddy and Momma noticed it, they didn't say anything. They just acted like everything was normal between the two of us. And maybe minus the squabbling, it was normal. I don't know what I'd expected from having the secret about the letter to hold over her head — but it wasn't this.

The next day, we had to register for school. Momma had already picked out my clothes, a navy blue skirt and a white blouse. As usual, I picked something else: a red T-shirt and a pair of jeans. After all, I'm ten years old and in the fifth grade. I don't know why Momma still picks out my clothes!

I put on my silver earrings that are shaped like

leaves. I liked to wear them because they remind me that things can blow away quickly — the bad and the good.

Daddy had already left for work by the time I got downstairs. Even though his job didn't start until 7:00 A.M., he left an hour early.

I was a little nervous. When you've changed schools as much as I have, you get used to meeting new people and learning a new place, but it's still a little scary.

All military schools are basically alike, and they're filled with all different kinds of kids. Everywhere you look, you see someone of a different nationality. Military kids get used to being shuffled around. Everybody knows how hard it is to come to school that first day, so most people are friendly and helpful there.

For the first time, I was going to attend a school where everyone had grown up in the same town, and in the same neighborhood. I'll bet most of the kids have known each other since kindergarten. I wondered if I'd be able to make new friends.

One thing I was sure of: I'd never have a friend like Annette.

I took one last look at myself and went downstairs to eat breakfast. I looked the same, but everything else was different.

# Chapter Four

## The New School

"Guess what, girls?" Momma said.

"What?" Sandra and I said at exactly the same moment. Real sisters would have held their pinkies out. But mean sisters like Sandra didn't go for that kind of stuff.

"I bet you're going to tell us where you found Sandra," I said, smiling.

"Found Sandra?" Momma asked, looking puzzled. "Found her where? When?"

"When she was left on the doorstep," I said.

"Please, don't start, Sharie. You and Sandra have been getting along so well these last few days."

Was she for real? Sandra hadn't spoken to me since the day of the robotic hug.

"I'm coming with the two of you to school today," Momma announced proudly.

I couldn't breathe. I shook my head. My ears can get so clogged up sometimes.

"And do you know why I'm coming?" Momma continued, smiling broadly.

"No," Sandra said, looking every bit as terrified as me.

"Because I haven't had a chance to take my babies to school since you were little. Now that I don't have to work, I'm going to volunteer in the library at Sharie's new elementary school and your new middle school at least once a week. Isn't that wonderful?"

Sandra and I just looked at each other. I could tell she hated the idea of Momma coming with us to school as much as I did. Momma hadn't gone to school with me since I was in kindergarten. She cried until they asked her to leave.

"You're joking, right, Momma?" Sandra said.

Momma tilted her head and narrowed her eyes. "Why would I be joking? Don't you want me to volunteer at your schools?"

Normally it would be me who'd blurt out something like "No, I sure don't," and hurt Momma's feelings. Then Sandra would come around the table being all mushy-mushy and hug Momma to cheer her up. I didn't say a word. I was proud of myself.

"Gosh, Momma," Sandra said. "This is a new school for me. I don't want to be called a baby because my momma comes to see me every week. Why can't you just stay at home and enjoy your new house? I'm not a baby anymore!"

Sandra threw her napkin on the table. Momma looked stunned and hurt.

I wanted to say, "See, Sandra, you hurt Momma's feelings," but nothing came out.

I couldn't believe Miss Perfect was acting this way. It was like watching *Tears and Joy,* Momma's favorite soap opera.

Momma stood up. "You better pick that napkin up, Sandra Anita Johnson, and fold it up neatly, and then apologize for your outburst."

I looked down at my plate. I felt confused inside. I should be happy to see Sandra in trouble. But I didn't feel that way. I wasn't sure what I felt, but it wasn't happiness. I didn't want Momma coming to my new school, either.

"Okay," Sandra said, picking up the napkin. "I'm sorry. But, Momma, you treat me like I'm a baby and I'm not. I'm growing up now."

"Yeah, well, you're not that grown. I've already signed up to volunteer at your schools. And that's what I'm going to do. Now, let's get ready to go."

When I saw my new school, I couldn't breathe. The school was huge. Even the sign that said CASEY ELEMENTARY SCHOOL had big letters. I stared at the kids running, walking, and riding their bikes toward the front double doors of the three-story brick building. We all got out of the car. I felt like my legs were frozen. I was glad Momma was with me after all.

"Momma," I said, "where are the other kids, you know, the Koreans, the Japanese, the African-Americans. . . ."

"I don't know," Momma said. "They're here somewhere, I'm sure. Just be patient."

Sandra said, "Are you sure, Momma? It doesn't look that way."

Sandra pulled Momma over to a bulletin board. The bulletin board was crammed full with photos of white kids.

"Come on," Momma said. "Don't worry about that now. Let's meet your new classmates and teachers."

We went into the principal's office. Dottie Riemer, the school principal, smiled when she saw Momma.

"Hello there, Mrs. Johnson," she said. "Good to see you again."

"Hello, Ms. Riemer," Momma said. "I want to introduce you to my girls. This is Sharie and this is Sandra."

Ms. Riemer had such a friendly smile that I couldn't help smiling back.

"Welcome to Casey!" Ms. Riemer said. "You're going to be in Ms. Susan Bailes' class. You'll love it! Come on, I'll show you the way."

" 'Bye, Sharie," Momma said. "I'm going to take Sandra to school, and then I'll be in the library, okay? Have a good day!"

I waved good-bye to Momma and Sandra. I followed Ms. Riemer up the stairs to my new class. Ms. Bailes was really nice. She introduced me to the class and told them that I had had a chance to travel to lots of places because my Dad was in the navy.

The other kids seemed impressed with the fact that I had lived in Japan, Germany, and six other states besides Texas. I was the only African-American girl in my class, but Ms. Bailes was so friendly that I didn't feel scared anymore.

After that first day, all the kids pretty much ignored me. No one was mean to me, but no one was really nice to me, either. I felt lonely and bored.

Every day was pretty much the same. I sat in class, answered questions sometimes, and sat by myself at lunch — or went in the library on Tuesdays or Thurs-

days, the days Momma was there as a volunteer. I was glad I had someone to talk to. I pretended everything was going great at school when I talked to Momma and Daddy. But I was sad, lonely, and bored. I missed Annette and my old school.

# Chapter Five

Me and My Big Mouth!

The first couple weeks of school weren't too bad — but they were about to get much, much worse. It started with the spelling bee. I'm a spelling bee champ, so I knew I would make it to the final round. And I did.

It was me versus Caitlin Mullen, the Queen of the Fifth Grade. She was the most popular girl at Casey. She wore her blond hair slicked back in a ponytail. She had the look that models in magazines have after somebody's painted over their faces with a brush — perfect. She wore neat sweaters and pants with perfect creases that ran from the top of her knees down to turned-up cuffs above her socks.

Did I mention she was smart, too? How do people

like Caitlin and Sandra get all the looks *and* all the brains?

Anyway, we were standing up in front of the class and everyone was staring at us. She had on a lavender blouse with ruffled sleeves, a black skirt, lavender socks, and black shoes.

Of course, this had been one of those days when I wasn't worried about what I wore. I'd thrown on the same crumpled T-shirt from the day before and my ripped jeans. I forgot my belt, so the jeans weren't fitting right. I had to hold them up with one hand while I tried to think of how the words were spelled.

On top of that, I'd gotten dressed with my eyes closed, something I do when I stay up too late and don't want to get up. I didn't notice that I was wearing one navy blue sock and a black sock with red lines in it until I got to school.

I spotted a few of the kids whispering and pointing down at my socks. I had to win or I'd never live it down. Besides, no one had ever beaten me in a spelling contest.

I looked over at Caitlin; she was fidgeting with her sleeve. I thought that was strange.

Ms. Bailes called out the word. "Melancholy, it means sadness or depression."

Without any hesitation at all I said, "M-e-l-a-c-h-l-y."

I smiled at Caitlin and whispered, "You can sit down now. I won!"

She lifted her wrist up to her face like she needed to wipe off sweat. Then she said, "I can spell it."

What was this? "I spelled it already. You got cotton in your ears?"

Some of the kids laughed.

"That wasn't correct, was it Ms. Bailes?" Caitlin asked.

I rolled my eyes. Some people will do anything to win.

"I'm afraid she's right, Sharie. That wasn't the correct spelling. Go on, Caitlin," Ms. Bailes said.

I felt a surge of heat in my stomach. I stared at Caitlin. She put her hand up to her face again and I spotted something sticking out from under her sleeve.

"M-e-l-a-n-c-h-o-l-y, melancholy," Caitlin said.

"We have a winner," Ms. Bailes said. "Congratulations, Caitlin! You get a free period to do whatever you want."

I glared at Caitlin. I could see something white sticking out from under one of the ruffles on her sleeve. I wanted to get a closer look. But instead, as usual, my big mouth opened and out popped two words. "She cheated."

"Did you hear that, Caitlin?" someone said. "Sharie called you a cheater."

I wanted to take it back. But it was too late.

Ms. Bailes stood up. "What do you mean? You think Caitlin cheated?"

"I did not," Caitlin shouted.

"Look under her sleeve," I said smugly. "She's got her cheat sheet tucked inside a bracelet or rubber band on her arm."

Caitlin shook her head. "You are so wrong."

"Yeah? Well, pull up your sleeve," I said. "Show us what you've got up there, Miss Spelling Magician."

"You two follow me," Ms. Bailes said.

"No, I want her to show everyone," I said. "Roll up your sleeve, Caitlin."

Ms. Bailes raised her eyebrows so high they blended into her hair. "I run this class, young lady."

"Yeah, well it's not fair for her to cheat," I said before I could stop myself. "She thinks she's queen of the class and queen of the spelling bee, but she's not!"

Okay, now I was on thin ice. I wanted to shut up, but my mouth kept right on going.

"Okay! Look," Caitlin said, shoving her sleeve up her arm. "I'm tired of you running off at the mouth when you don't know what you're talking about."

It was a fancy white lace handkerchief tucked into an elastic wristband. "My grandmother makes me wear it this way. She says it's the ladylike way to take care of your nose. Are you satisfied now?"

"Sorry, Caitlin," I whispered. I wanted to run away and hide.

"Sharie, come with me," Ms. Bailes said, pointing to me. "Everyone else take out your math books and do the problems on page twenty-six."

Oh, no! I was in big trouble now. Why did I have to talk so much?

I marched behind Ms. Bailes into the hallway. She gave me a lecture about not accusing people before I had all the facts. She told me that she wanted me to go back to my desk and write, "I will not speak until I have all the facts" 500 times and turn it in tomorrow. She also told me to write a note of apology to Caitlin.

With every line I wrote I promised myself that from now on I was going to keep my mouth shut. That promise lasted until lunchtime. We were in the cafeteria when a boy called me "Queen Bee," then he made a buzzing sound. Everyone in the lunch line started to laugh.

Ms. Bailes walked over and said, "Be quiet. All of you."

The giggling stopped.

Then out of the quietness I heard, "I think it isn't so strange that Sharie accused Caitlin of cheating. After all, Caitlin was looking at her sleeve and it makes sense that Sharie thought she was cheating. Who here wouldn't have said the same thing?"

Everyone's head whipped in the same direction, toward the back of our line. It was Hannah Lowenstein again, the second most talked-about girl in our class, after me.

There she stood, tall and lean, with her red bushy hair standing all over her head like a wild woman from some movie, defending me. Her legs were covered with a purple sock on one leg and a candy-striped sock on the other. Her shirt jingled every time she moved because she had bells tied on it. Her skirt had different kinds of patches with slogans on them, like "Conserve Water!" and "SMILE!" Hannah Lowenstein stood there sticking up for me with one white tennis shoe and one green tennis shoe, just like she was doing me a favor. I could bet not one person was listening because they were all too busy staring at her outfit.

That day in the cafeteria, I hurried to get my food so I could sit down and get away from everyone. I spotted an empty chair. By the time I got there it was taken. I walked toward another table where there were two empty chairs.

"I'm saving this seat," the girl who was sitting there said.

Our class had to sit together. So far, every day I'd ended up sitting at a table alone. "You're not supposed to save seats," I said.

"Why, you going to tell Ms. Bailes, tattletale, or are you going to accuse us of cheating you out of a seat?"

I walked away. I sat down at an empty table next to the class.

"May I join you?" someone said.

I looked up with a smile. Then I saw Hannah in her crazy outfit and I stopped smiling.

"Sure," I said. "Sit down."

I noticed everyone was whispering and pointing at us. I pretended that I didn't care. Oh, well. Having Hannah Lowenstein sit with me was better than sitting alone. I don't care about clothes, but Hannah was too way out there for me. I liked to blend in, but Hannah loved to stand out in a crowd.

I wanted to ask her why she dressed like that. But before I could say anything, she spoke up.

"Hey, I liked that little story you read the other

day. You know, the one about your grandmother. I thought it was neat the way you read it as if you were all four people."

"Thank you," I said. I had written the story in parts, like a play. I was all four voices; my grandma's, mine, my sister's, and my mother's voice. No one else had complimented me on it, except Ms. Bailes.

"I like acting myself. I might be an actress one day. I close my eyes sometimes and I can see my name in lights. See," she said. Hannah opened her jacket. Lights flashed on and off. I blinked. Hannah had her name spelled out on this little pin on her shirt. When she pushed a button, her name lit up. I shook my head. This was one weird girl.

"You want to eat with me again tomorrow?" she asked.

I didn't know what to say. I knew I wouldn't become popular hanging out with Hannah Lowenstein. But no one else at this school had tried to be friends with me.

"Sure," I said. "We can eat lunch together tomorrow."

"Good," she said, standing up. "Ciao, Bella."

"Huh? Oh, yeah. Chow, Bella," I said. I didn't speak Italian, but I knew greetings from many countries. In military school you learn different greetings for the students from other countries. In my last school, we learned to say hello and good-bye in Japanese, French, German, Vietnamese, and Italian. For weeks everyone walked around saying, "Chow."

I watched Hannah leave the lunchroom. Where was she going?

I quickly put my tray away and followed her to the bathroom. She stood in front of the mirror talking to herself. She was pretending to be interviewed. She asked herself the questions and then gave the answers back to the mirror. She didn't even care that the other girls in the bathroom were laughing at her. I washed my hands and left. That girl is weird, weird, weird, I thought.

# Chapter Six

Big Fat Lies

That evening, I tried to do my homework, but I couldn't concentrate. This was the first time I'd gone to a school that I didn't love. I liked Ms. Bailes, but the kids didn't seem to like me.

I picked up my English book. We were on Chapter 4. Our assignment was to write three declarative paragraphs on three different topics. I sat staring at the computer. Nothing popped into my head. I read the assignment again. Hmmm. I picked up my Game Boy. I played until I heard Momma calling us to dinner. After dinner, I played until it was time to go to bed. It wasn't that I didn't think about my homework, I just didn't feel like doing it. But I couldn't stop playing the game.

I played game after game until Daddy knocked on the door and told me to go to sleep. I knew I was going to be in trouble, but I tried not to think about it.

The next day when Ms. Bailes asked us to turn in our homework, I was the only person who didn't have the assignment.

"Where is your homework, Sharie?" Ms. Bailes asked after she'd collected all the papers.

I couldn't think of anything to say. "I don't know where it is," I said.

"What do you mean you don't know where it is?"

I shrugged. "I mean, I don't know where it is."

"Did you do it?" Ms. Bailes asked.

Now was the moment I didn't prepare for and a lie sprang out of my mouth. "Yes, I did it."

"Then where is it?" Ms. Bailes asked.

"I lost it," I lied again.

Ms. Bailes sighed loudly. "You lost your homework. Where did you have it last?"

"If I knew that, I could probably find it." I didn't

mean to say that. I rolled my eyes at myself. Be quiet, Sharie.

Ms. Bailes said, "Don't get smart with me, young lady. And do not roll your eyes at me."

"I wasn't rolling my eyes at you," I said. Momma would ground me until I was eighteen if I got into any more trouble.

"You're skating on thin ice, Sharie," Ms. Bailes said.

I wanted to stop. Honestly. I hadn't even thought of anything to say back. But words floated out of my mouth. "No wonder it's so cold in here."

"Sharie, come with me," Ms. Bailes said.

"That girl stays in trouble," a boy named Brad Strickland said under his breath.

Hannah Lowenstein said, "No, she doesn't."

I followed Ms. Bailes out into the hall.

"I've read your records, Sharie. Up until now you've been a good student. No behavior problems. What is happening to you?"

I shrugged. I really didn't know what was happening to me.

"You need to answer me, sweetie," Ms. Bailes said.

I looked up at her. She wasn't being mean. I was about to cry. "I don't know what's the matter with me," I whispered.

"Well, let's work on your attitude. And you must stop talking back. Now, let's go back inside. And tomorrow I expect you to bring me the homework you lost. Okay?"

"Okay," I said. "May I go to the bathroom to wipe my face?" I asked, wiping tears with the back of my hand. I sniffled.

"Sure. Come right back." She handed me a pass from her pocket.

I stared at myself in the bathroom mirror. Ms. Bailes was right. I had never been in trouble at school before. And I always turned in my homework. What was wrong with me?

After school I promised myself that I was going to go straight home and do my homework. I would do the assignment from yesterday first and then the new assignments. I pulled out my English, math, and science books. I lined them up in order. I would do the English assignments first. I opened my book to Chapter 4. I read the assignment sheet. Suddenly, I felt thirsty.

I drank a big glass of juice and ate a piece of cheese and some crackers.

"How's everything going?" Momma asked me. "You're being awful quiet about school. Do you like it?"

"I love it," I lied. I was in no mood to talk.

"That's wonderful," Momma said. "Your father and I were beginning to worry. You normally can't stop talking about school and your friends. Have you made any new friends?"

"Yes, I've made new friends. I'm very popular," I lied again. I had been lying all day. I wondered if my nose was going to start growing like Pinocchio's did. "I've got a lot of homework to do. I better get back to it."

I hurried back to my room. I didn't work on my homework. I picked up my Game Boy and began to play. I played until dinner, and then I started on my homework. I did a few of the questions and then I started to play on the Game Boy again. I couldn't seem to stop.

When Ms. Bailes found out that I didn't have any of my assignments, she called me out into the hall.

"I'm going to contact your mother. I think she should know what terrible calamities continue to happen to your homework," Ms. Bailes said.

I could tell by her expression and raised eyebrows that she knew I had been lying to her about the homework. I couldn't believe it myself. I wasn't a liar.

Now I was in big trouble. I'd told Momma that Ms. Bailes was out sick. I said that the substitute wasn't giving us homework. I was busted.

I could barely eat my dinner. I kept waiting for the phone to ring. When it finally rang, I jumped up quickly and ran into the kitchen to answer it.

"I'll get it," I said.

I could hear Momma say, "That must be one of her new friends calling her."

Daddy said, "Calling during dinner? She needs to tell them that this is when we eat together as a family."

"Hello," I said, breathing like a dragon. I didn't know what I would say, but I had to think of something to keep Momma from the telephone.

"Hey, it's me, Hannah."

My shoulders relaxed. "Hey, Hannah. I'm glad it's you."

"Great. My mother wants to know if I can come over on Saturday. She's going out of town and I told her I don't want to go to a baby-sitter's. She still calls it a baby-sitter, not me."

"I have to ask my parents," I said.

"Momma, can I have a friend over on Saturday?" I yelled.

Momma stood behind me. "I'm right here. Don't scream. Let me speak to your friend's parent," Momma said, motioning for the telephone.

"My momma wants to talk to your mother first," I said.

I watched Momma talking to Mrs. Lowenstein. Daddy called me from the dining room. I wanted to hear what Momma was saying, but I knew Daddy wanted to talk to me right away.

"Yes, Daddy," I said.

"You need to tell your friends that we eat dinner between six P.M. and seven P.M., every weeknight."

"Yes, sir. I will," I said as I started eating again.

"Sounds like you found a nice friend," Momma said.

"Uh-huh," I said.

I wouldn't call Hannah a close friend, not yet anyway. Not like Annette. I wondered if Momma would think so highly of Hannah once she saw that she dressed like a circus clown.

"Hannah's going to spend the night Saturday while her mother is out of town," Momma said.

"Not spend the night," I said quickly. "She's just coming over for awhile."

"I told her mother she could spend the night," Momma said. "That way her mother doesn't have to rush back home. Besides, I thought you'd want to have company. You always loved for Annette to spend the night."

"That was different," I said. "Annette was my best friend."

"So, Hannah can be your best friend here."

"Yeah, you and that girl Hannah can be weirdos together," Sandra said.

"What do you mean?" Daddy said.

"I mean this girl is really strange, that's all."

"Stop it, Sandra," I said. "No one is any stranger than you. At least she's from earth."

"Please, don't start," Momma said.

The phone rang again.

I jumped up, knocking my water glass over. Water spilled across the tablecloth and dripped onto the floor.

"I'll get it," Daddy said. "Sit down and eat your dinner. If this is another one of your friends, I need to have a chat with them."

If that was Ms. Bailes and Daddy talked to her first, I was really in hot water. Momma handled problems totally differently from Daddy. If Ms. Bailes told Momma about my not doing homework and lying, she would probably just talk to me about it and make me do the work. But I really didn't know what Daddy would say. When he was in the navy, Momma always handled our punishment if we did something wrong.

I couldn't hear Daddy saying anything. I prayed that it wasn't Ms. Bailes. Maybe it was one of Daddy's friends. I pushed my food around on my plate. I was so nervous that I couldn't eat.

"Don't you like your dinner, Sharie?" Momma asked.

"Yes, it's good," I said.

I tried to eat a few bites of my vegetables. I could hear Daddy hanging up the phone in the kitchen.

When he finally walked back into the dining room, I knew he'd been talking to Ms. Bailes. He looked really mad.

"May I see you in the bedroom?" he asked Momma.

I held my head down. My chin almost rested on my chest. I couldn't look at him. I heard Momma getting up from the chair, asking, "What's the matter? What is it?"

"What did you do now?" Sandra asked. "Whatever it is, you're in big trouble if Daddy stopped eating to have a meeting with Momma. I'd hate to be in your shoes."

"As if you could put those big feet in my shoes," I said. "Leave me alone."

"Let me see," Sandra said slowly. "I think you'll probably be grounded until your prom night. Oh, wait, no one would invite you to the prom, anyway."

"Be quiet!" I screamed just in time for Momma and Daddy to hear me.

"Stop shouting at your sister," Momma said as she walked into the room.

I held my head down again. I could see the disappointment all over her face.

"That was your teacher on the phone," Daddy said. "I cannot believe you, young lady. What on earth has gotten into you?"

I didn't answer. I tried dropping my chin lower.

Daddy walked back and forth, talking about the importance of education. Then Momma said they would visit the school on Friday and that there would be new rules about my schoolwork.

"As soon as you get home, you can eat a snack

and then do your homework," Daddy said. "Either Momma or I will check it. No Game Boy until your grades are higher."

"Hannah can visit on Saturday since I promised her mother that she could come," Momma said. "But after that no more company until your grades improve."

"I'm sorry," I said.

"We're really disappointed that you've been lying, Sharie," Momma said.

I felt terrible. What was the matter with me? I couldn't believe the trouble I'd gotten myself into.

# Chapter Seven

## The Sleepover

The next day at school, I kept quiet the entire day. I only spoke when I was spoken to. I felt angry and upset. I wasn't mad at Momma, Daddy, or Ms. Bailes. I was mad at myself. As soon as I got home, I worked on my homework. It took a long time to finish everything because I was so far behind. Momma checked it for me. As soon as I made a few corrections, I went to bed. I was glad the week was over.

On Saturday, Daddy decided to paint the inside of the garage gray. I think the dark gray color reminds him of his old ship. I helped Daddy paint for awhile. He told me funny stories about being in the navy. It made me feel better that he wasn't mad at me.

Hannah and her mother showed up around noon. I thought Hannah's mother would dress and look like Hannah. I was wrong. Mrs. Lowenstein looked like a model playing the part of a business executive. She wore a beautiful navy blue suit with matching navy blue high-heeled shoes. Her red hair was smooth, straight, and cut in a short, sleek hairstyle. Hannah was wearing a huge striped sweater that hung down to her knees and a pair of jeans with a hole in one knee. She had braided part of her hair and had left the rest in a curly red mass that spiked up wildly all over her head. She was carrying some kind of cage.

"Hey, Hannah," I said. "What's that?"

"Howdy, hello!" Hannah said. "This is my crabitat and this is Herman and Sherman, my hermit crabs."

Momma told Hannah's mom that she was happy that we had become friends.

"Yes, I think their friendship is just wonderful," Mrs. Lowenstein said. "Hannah is so unusually mature. Most children don't understand her."

Hannah looked embarrassed.

"Let's go up to my room," I said quickly.

"Okay," Hannah said. " 'Bye, Mom. Have a good trip."

"Good-bye, dear," Hannah's mother said.

Hannah loved my room. She looked at my posters, my books, and my CDs. We took Herman and Sherman out of the crabitat. Hannah showed me how to hold my hands close together over the bed so that they could crawl safely and have a soft place to land if they fell. Herman tickled my hands as he crawled across my palms.

"I'm allergic to dogs and cats, so Herman and Sherman are the perfect pets," Hannah said.

"Maybe my parents will let me have a pair of crabs," I said.

"Maybe. They're really fun to watch and they're not that hard to take care of," Hannah said.

Hannah put Herman back into the crabitat. I liked playing with Sherman. He seemed to like me.

Hannah flipped through my CDs. We discovered that we liked the same kinds of music. She put on a CD and danced around the room, her wild, red hair flying everywhere. I laughed until my sides ached.

"What's this?" Hannah asked as she flopped down into the chair by my desk and looked at my papers. "Hey, this is good!"

I put Sherman down on the bed and went over to my desk.

Hannah was looking at a play I'd written called *The Outside Girl*. I was excited that she liked it, and we decided to act it out. Hannah read the main parts and I read all the other characters. We screamed and laughed and shouted like they do onstage.

Finally, Sandra said, "Momma, please make them stop screaming."

"Girls, tone it down, please," Momma said.

"Okay, Momma," I said.

It was time for a snack anyway, so we went to the kitchen. Hannah and I sliced up a pile of cheese and got a box of crackers and some juice boxes.

"Who cut the cheese?" I said.

We laughed so hard that juice bubbled out of our mouths. That made us completely hysterical. Finally, Momma told us it was time to get ready for bed.

"Okay," I said.

"Good night, Mrs. Johnson," Hannah said.

"Good night, girls," Momma said.

On our way upstairs, I whispered to Hannah. "She said get ready for bed — she didn't say go to bed!"

Hannah giggled. We were in our pajamas snacking on crackers when I had a great idea.

"You know what?" I said. "We should start an acting club at school."

"That's a fabulous idea," Hannah said, grinning.

We squealed and jumped around congratulating ourselves and pretending we were famous. I made a gown out of my bedsheet and walked around like a movie star. Hannah got my autograph. Then I asked her for hers.

"You can be the president, since it's your idea, and I'll be the vice president," Hannah said, writing on the pad.

"Sounds great. Let's make a notice on the computer. Are we letting anyone in or should we have rules and regulations?"

"I think we should have rules," Hannah said. "For

the first rule, they have to be interested in serious acting."

I nodded. "Yes, and they must come to meetings and practice. We'll do two or three plays a year."

"Speedo," Hannah said.

I'd noticed that Hannah makes up her own words when she wants to say something is "cool." I'd gotten used to it, but some of the kids in our class thought it was a weird thing to do.

"Do you want to do my play first?" I asked. I didn't want to seem too pushy, but I thought I had written a good play. And I could see Hannah in the leading role.

My play was about a girl who didn't have many friends because she didn't fit in. I'd worked really hard on it and I was happy that Hannah liked it so much.

"I'll direct it, of course."

Hannah jumped up, clapped her hands, and spun around and around.

"I can play Tina, the leading lady." Hannah

bowed. "Thank you, thank you very much," she said, pretending she had a huge audience.

"We can make a sign for auditions, too," I said. We sat down at the computer.

"This is going to be great!" I said.

"Fabuliciously grandido," Hannah said.

"Yeah." I typed:

SOMETHING NEW TO DO!
Join the ACTING CLUB today. Be onstage tomorrow! Our membership is open to all serious actors and other people interested in the world of theater. Bad actors need not apply!

When we finished, we admired our signs. The last line was Hannah's idea. Our audition sign was more to the point.

AUDITIONS, AUDITIONS, AUDITIONS!
for Casey Elementary School's First
Professional Play

THE OUTSIDE GIRL
Written and directed by
SHARIE JOHNSON
Openings for ten parts
This Friday after school

We typed a sign-up form for people to fill out with their names, phone numbers and addresses, and the parts they wanted to play.

"This is a great idea!" Hannah said. "It's the best thing that ever happened at Casey!"

"Of course, we have to get approval for the club and the audition from Ms. Bailes and Ms. Riemer," I said.

"Right!" Hannah agreed.

"And we'll probably have to get permission to use the school auditorium for our meetings, the auditions, and the play," I said.

"Easy," Hannah said.

"Oh, and we'll need permission to put on the play."

"No problemo! Don't worry about a thing!" Hannah said. "My mom's on the school board. She'll help us get permission for everything we need!"

We both screamed and jumped up and down.

"Girls," Daddy said. "Go to bed, now!"

"Yes, sir!" we said.

Hannah held her hand over her mouth to smother her giggles. I put my head under the covers so Daddy wouldn't hear me laughing. I don't even remember falling asleep.

# Chapter Eight

## My New Friends

We slept late the next morning. I made up my bed and then threw a pillow at Hannah so she'd wake up. She threw it back at me and we had a pillow fight until Sandra started yelling at us to be quiet.

We went downstairs to get some breakfast. Momma and Daddy were still asleep. Daddy works such long hours that he doesn't get up for "field days" anymore. We're all glad.

Hannah's mom was coming to pick her up in an hour, so we rushed around getting dressed and cleaning up my room.

The doorbell rang.

"That's my mom," Hannah said. "Time to go, little crabs."

Hannah picked up her crabitat and peered inside. "Where's Sherman?" Hannah asked.

"Isn't he in there?" I asked.

"No," Hannah said. "You were playing with him last night. Didn't you put him back in the crabitat?"

"I, I can't remember," I said.

"Well, he's got to be around here somewhere," Hannah said.

We looked all over my room for Sherman. I could hear Momma talking with Mrs. Lowenstein.

"Hannah," Momma said. "Your mom's here."

"I'm coming," Hannah said. "Call me as soon as you find Sherman. He'll come out of his hiding place soon."

"I will," I promised.

Hannah hugged me. "Let's be best friends, okay?"

I didn't know what to say, so I didn't say anything. Hannah looked a little hurt.

"Hannah!" Momma said. "Your mother needs to go now!"

"Okay," Hannah said.

"'Bye, Hannah," I said. "I'll call you as soon as I find Sherman."

"Okay," Hannah said. "I had fun."

"Me, too," I said.

Hannah ran downstairs. I looked out the window and waved to her as she got into the car. After Hannah left, I decided to e-mail Annette.

To be honest, I had started to feel a little disloyal to her. After all, before I left Kansas, I promised Annette that *she* would always be my very best friend. But I liked Hannah and I wanted to be her best friend, too. I wasn't sure if one person could have two best friends. I typed a quick e-mail to Annette.

Hey, Annette,

You are still and always will be my best, closest, forever friend. I miss you very much. I can't wait until this summer because Momma said we might go back to Kansas for a visit. I hope so. How's school? My new school is okay. It's kind of strange because no one has a parent in the military. I've made a good friend here. Her name is Hannah. Can one person have two best friends? Let me know.

Your best buddy,
Sharie

I thought about saying something about our new acting club, but I didn't. I'll tell her about the play when we are ready to put it on. Maybe I can send her a video. That would be better.

I had just finished sending my e-mail when I heard a strange sound in my trash can. Something was rustling around in there! I slowly pulled the trash can out from under my desk and looked inside.

"Sherman!"

Sherman was clinging to a cracker. He looked just fine.

"Boy, am I glad to see you!" I said.

I found a deep box to put Sherman in while I called Hannah to tell her the good news. Her mother answered the phone and said that Hannah was at a music lesson. She said she would come right over with Hannah's crabitat to pick up Sherman.

"Thanks, Mrs. Lowenstein," I said.

Mrs. Lowenstein arrived so quickly that I barely had time to play with Sherman. I carefully placed him in his crabitat and locked the door to the cage.

"See you later, Sherman," I said. "Tell Hannah I say hello. Thanks for picking him up, Mrs. Lowenstein."

"No. Thank you," Mrs. Lowenstein said. "Hannah has a hard time making friends. I'm so pleased that you're best friends and have so much in common."

"Oh, yes," I stammered. "I'm glad, too."

Oh, well. Hannah seemed determined to be my best friend even if I wasn't sure if I was hers.

On Monday morning before school started, I talked to Ms. Bailes about the acting club and my play. She said she would support it if I promised to improve my grades. Even though I made up my homework, I had failed the last two tests. I had never made a grade below a B before, but now my mind would go blank whenever I had a test. I promised

Ms. Bailes I would study harder and bring up my grades.

Hannah and I made an appointment to talk with Ms. Riemer, the principal, during lunch. We told her all about the acting club, the auditions, and my play. Hannah even acted out some of the parts. Ms. Riemer loved our idea and told us we could post our signs announcing the club and the auditions around the school.

After we left the principal's office, Hannah and I covered our mouths to keep from screaming. It was all set. We were going to put on my play at Casey Elementary!

Hannah and I put up our signs all over the school. After school, we had a big crowd waiting to get the forms for joining the club. Hannah explained all the parts for the play. We passed out the parts so people could study for the audition on Friday.

Each day more and more people asked about the club and the play. I realized that I was almost popular. When I walked into the cafeteria now, people actually

called to me to sit with them. I just smiled and said that I was going to sit with Hannah.

On Thursday, Hannah told me she would be late coming to lunch because she needed to stop by the library first.

As soon as I picked up my lunch tray, I heard someone calling my name.

"Hey, want to sit with us, Sharie?" someone asked.

I turned around. It was Caitlin Mullen and the two girls she hung out with, Anysa Bailey and Karly Norris. They were definitely the most popular girls in the fifth grade. Caitlin Mullen, Queen Caitlin, was asking me if I wanted to sit with them. I didn't move. I probably looked silly just standing there staring at them.

"Here, let me help you with your tray," Caitlin said, taking the tray from my hands. "I'm glad you're by yourself and not with that Hannah."

I sat down beside Caitlin. I know I should have said something to defend Hannah, but I was speechless. I was so surprised that she wanted me to sit with them that I didn't say a word.

"Listen," Caitlin said, "I read your play. It's really good."

"It sure is," Karly said.

That made me smile. I don't know why. Caitlin hadn't exactly been friendly to me until now. And since I accused her of cheating, she was always making some smart remark about me. Now I was thrilled to be sitting with her and her friends. Here I was, Sharie Johnson, sitting with the most popular girls in the fifth grade. I'd never been part of the most popular crowd at school, ever!

"We want to join your acting club on Friday," Caitlin continued. "Did you know that I took acting classes last summer? I had the lead role in *Romeo and Juliet*. I think your play is just as good as anything Shakespeare wrote."

"You do?" I said, almost breathless. "You're kidding me, right?"

"No way." She turned to Anysa. "Didn't I tell you that?"

"She sure did," Anysa said. "I loved your play, too!

I'll bet you're going to be a famous writer when you grow up!"

"Oh, well, thanks, thank you," I said, stuttering.

I didn't care if Caitlin was just buttering me up. I knew my play couldn't be as good as Shakespeare's. I didn't say it, though. I just sat there feeling very proud.

Suddenly, Hannah appeared at the head of the table. "Hey, what are you doing sitting here?" she said. "Come on, let's find a seat."

I looked up. Her hair seemed even wilder and redder today.

"What? Oh, come on, sit with us," I said, almost too low for anyone to hear.

"There's no room," Caitlin said quickly. "Sorry."

Hannah glared at me. "Are you coming or not, Sharie?"

"Pull that chair from over there," I said. "You can squeeze in beside me."

I hoped Hannah would just go ahead and sit down instead of making such a fuss. Hannah didn't move. I didn't move, either.

"Never mind. I'll just sit over there," Hannah said slowly. "I have to hurry, anyway."

I watched her walk away. I felt like a worm. Why didn't I get up? What was wrong with me? I could see that Hannah was hurt and disappointed. She looked lonely sitting at our table all by herself. I started to get up when Caitlin grabbed my arm and pulled me back down into my chair.

"Guess what, Sharie. I'm having a party Saturday," Caitlin said. "Everybody who's anybody will be there. And guess who's going to be my special guest."

"You won't believe it," Anysa said. "You won't guess in a million years."

Hannah watched me from two tables away. I pretended I didn't see her staring at me.

"Is it someone from school?" I asked.

"Nope, they're not from school. Try harder. It's somebody famous," Caitlin said.

"I don't think I can guess," I said, but what I really meant was I couldn't think. I looked over at Hannah again. She wouldn't look at me.

"It's Little James, the singer," Caitlin, Anysa, and Karly screamed in unison.

My mouth gaped open. "Really? Little James is coming to your house for the party?" I shook my head in disbelief. "No way," I said.

"Yes, he's singing just for me!" Caitlin said. "My daddy is an entertainment lawyer and he got his friend to set this up for my birthday. Cool, huh?"

This was way more than cool. I couldn't wait to tell Sandra. She would die with envy. I was invited to a party with Little James! Then I saw Hannah out of the corner of my eye. She looked lonely. I cleared my throat.

"What about Hannah?" I said. "She's invited, too, right?"

Without one second of hesitation, Caitlin, Anysa, and Karly all said, "No way!"

I stared at them. Did they just say, No?

Caitlin said quickly, "It's not that we don't like Hannah or anything, but I can only invite so many people. And I'm sorry, but the guest list is full."

I sat there staring down at my fingernails. They

were plain, no polish. One of them even had a little dirt under it. I glanced over at the other girls' nails. They all had professional manicures, polished and sparkling.

I wanted to say that if Hannah couldn't come, I wouldn't be coming, either. But instead I heard myself saying, "What are you going to wear?"

Caitlin talked on and on about the special outfit she was going to buy at the mall. I just smiled, nodded my head, and tried not to look at Hannah.

It was in that moment that I understood that somehow I was changing. I, loyal Sharie, was no longer a good friend. I wondered if I would have spoken up for Annette. Of course I would have, I told myself, while half listening to the girls talk about what they were planning to wear to meet Little James. After all, I never told Hannah that she was my best friend. She just said that I was hers.

# Chapter Nine

The Party

That night, I pretended to be busy when Hannah called. At dinner, I told Momma and Daddy about the party. As I expected, Sandra pretended not to care that I had been invited to a party — until I said Little James would be there. Suddenly, Sandra was listening to me.

"I want to go, too, Momma," she said.

"She can't go," I said. "Caitlin said no one else could come. Honest." I smiled as I said this.

For once, I was going to do something that Miss Prissy Sandra couldn't do. Momma said she would buy me a new outfit to wear.

Then she said, "I bet Hannah will even dress like

a young lady for this one. What is she wearing?" Momma asked.

I hated to tell her. I said, "Caitlin said she didn't have any more invitations, so Hannah can't make it."

Daddy raised his eyebrows. "Really? And you're still going?"

"Daddy, it isn't my fault Hannah isn't going. Why should I miss the party? Hannah doesn't even want to go."

I didn't know that for a fact, but I couldn't recall Hannah ever mentioning liking Little James' music. Of course, I had never mentioned him, either.

"Who is this Little James, anyway?" Momma said.

"He was in the movie that we watched, remember?" I said. "You know, the movie where the boy helped all the animals in the forest by singing that magic song?"

"You said you didn't like it that much, Momma. Plus, Little James is a rapper," Sandra said.

Daddy's fork stopped in midair. "Oh, you didn't tell us that."

"Daddy, Sandra is just mad because she isn't going. You didn't hear her telling you he was a rapper when she thought she could go, did you?"

Momma nodded. "She has a point, Sandra. Now finish your dinner."

"Are boys going to be at this party?" Daddy asked.

"I don't know, Daddy," I said. "I don't care about boys, anyway. P.S. Sandra is the one who likes boys."

I smiled and made kissing noises.

Sandra glared at me. Then she remembered that P.S. on the letter from Robert Nichols that I still had. She tried to kick me under the table. I moved my legs out of the way.

"Okay," Daddy said. "You can go, but I'm going to call the Mullens and make sure that they will have chaperones at this party."

"They will," I said.

Yeah! I was on my way to the most popular girl in the fifth grade's party. And I was going to meet Little James. Best of all, thanks to the acting club, I was finally making friends at school.

On Friday afternoon, a crowd showed up for the

audition and the meeting. I couldn't believe that so many kids were interested.

I had each person go up onstage to audition. They told the audience which part they wanted to play. Caitlin, Anysa, Karly, and Hannah were the only ones who had had acting experience.

Hannah seemed shyer than I thought she would be when she walked up onstage. She had on a multi-colored dress made out of bedsheets. She'd cut them up so that she looked sort of like a rag doll, especially with her wild red hair.

She said she'd been in several plays at her syna-gogue, including the *Diary of Anne Frank,* in which she played the star. She read the part of Tina perfectly. I saw two people clap other than me. I wrote Tina's name down beside hers. That was final. Hannah was my leading lady. Maybe choosing her for the lead part would make up for her not being invited to Caitlin's party. I smiled at Hannah and gave her a thumbs-up. She smiled back.

Then it was Caitlin's turn. She went to the center of the stage and smiled at the audience.

"I want to play Tina, the leading lady's part. If you look at my bio, you'll see that I have six years of acting experience and have been in three leading lady roles."

How could somebody only ten years old have six years of acting experience? Oh, no! This was going to be a problem. I didn't even want to think about it. Now I wished I'd gotten someone else to decide who would play each part. But oh, no, I just had to have the control. Well, now I had it and no matter what I did, someone was going to be mad at me.

Hannah looked like she was going to burst. She watched my face while Tina, I mean, Caitlin, read her lines. She even managed to cry at the right time. Real tears were dripping down her face!

Caitlin was really, really good. Everyone clapped when she finished. She wiped away her tears, smiled sweetly, and sank into a deep bow, folding one leg under the other dramatically, dipping her head to the floor.

I didn't know what to do. Why did Caitlin have to be so good at everything? Why?

I told everyone I'd assign the parts and let them know my decision on the following Tuesday. I added that I had a busy weekend because I was going to Caitlin's party to meet Little James, just in case someone at school didn't know about it. Everyone knew about it. Caitlin's party was the only thing anyone talked about. Some of the kids in our class had started teasing Hannah when they found out I was invited to the party and she wasn't.

Hannah stopped speaking to me the day after I sat with Caitlin in the cafeteria. I kept trying to get Hannah to sit with us, but she walked past me like I was invisible. Some people are too stubborn for their own good. Maybe if she were a little nicer to Caitlin she would have gotten invited to the party, too. I tried not to look at Hannah during lunch. It made me feel bad.

On Saturday, Momma curled my hair all over so that I would look pretty for Caitlin's party. I had a new pair of jeans and a shiny, purple top to wear to the party. I put on a pair of silver hoop earrings and a bunch of silver bracelets.

I went into Sandra's room while she was downstairs and used some of her lip gloss and perfume. Then I went downstairs.

When Daddy saw me, he whistled. "Wow, look at you, baby. You look really grown-up. And you're so cute," he said, pinching my cheek.

Sandra sniffed the air. "Is that my perfume you're wearing?"

I didn't even respond to her. I just smiled. There was nothing she could do about it, anyway.

"Hey, bring me back an autograph," she said as I walked out the door with Momma.

"I'll see what I can do," I said, smiling. I was going to get her one, but I thought I'd let her sweat a little.

Momma dropped me off at Caitlin's and I waved good-bye as I ran up to the house. I couldn't wait to get inside to see Little James.

The party wasn't as much fun as I thought it was going to be. Now, here I was sitting on a hard chair and listening to Caitlin and her buddies make fun of people. Little James didn't even show up.

Caitlin's father apologized. "Little James had a schedule change at the last minute. But I'll make it up to Caitlin. He promised me that when he does his next movie, she could be on the set."

Caitlin was happy. But I doubt if anyone else was. We weren't going to the set.

As I listened to Caitlin, Anysa, and Karly giggle about everything, I realized that I was feeling sad. Have you ever done something you knew you shouldn't have done? You know, like sneaked in someplace you weren't supposed to be or eaten your momma's last piece of chocolate candy? Caitlin's party turned out to be like that for me. I couldn't enjoy myself because I was thinking about Hannah. To be honest I missed Hannah a lot. She was funny, kind, and rarely gossiped about people, unlike Caitlin and her friends. If I had a dollar for every time they talked about someone, I could have bought a new computer game.

I realized Hannah was a lot like Annette. Annette didn't gossip, either. We both had plenty to do besides talk about other people.

When Momma finally came to pick me up, I was glad. I hadn't talked to anyone the entire time. Caitlin pulled me around like a pet poodle for awhile when the party began. But by the time her father made the announcement that Little James wasn't coming, I think she'd forgotten I was there.

I was about to follow Momma out the door when Caitlin ran over to say good-bye. At least I thought she came to say good-bye, but instead she said, "I hope I get the part of Tina."

"I hope so, too," I said, wishing I didn't even have to think about it. What was I going to do? No matter who I chose for the part, someone was going to be mad at me.

There are times when something that seems bad turns out to be a good thing. I thought Daddy's new job would mean he was around all the time, forcing us to do hours of housework, but that didn't happen. Now it was more like old times. Daddy was fun again. We took long walks together in the afternoon. I wanted to tell him about what had been happening between Hannah and me. But then I'd have to admit

I went to the party even though I knew she hadn't been invited. Daddy believed in loyalty; it was the navy way.

I didn't think he would understand my choosing to go to the party without Hannah. So we walked and talked about everything but what I really wanted to talk about.

The thing about parents is that as long as you're talking to them, they're happy. Sometimes they can be so clueless. Just because someone is talking doesn't mean they're saying what they need to say. I had no one to turn to.

Annette wrote to me every week at first. Now I was lucky if it was once a month. To be honest, I couldn't even be mad at her since I hadn't written to her much once I started hanging around with Caitlin and her friends. I realized I still called Anysa and Karly, "Caitlin's friends." That's funny, since we spent all day together. You'd think I would feel like they were my friends, too, but I didn't.

I was changing and I didn't like it. I had to get myself back on track. Choosing Caitlin instead of Hannah for the lead role in the play wouldn't do it. I tossed and turned all night. I had chosen someone for every single part except for the leading lady.

On Monday morning, I stood in the mirror combing my hair when it hit me. Maybe I can convince Caitlin she doesn't really want to be Tina. After all, Tina's not such a nice person until the end of the play. Yes, that was it.

By second period I had come up with a plan. If it didn't work, everyone would be mad at me!

# Chapter Ten

## Miss Popularity

At lunch, before I could say anything, Caitlin said, "Guess what, Sharie."

"What?" I said.

"I heard that Hannah Lowenstein said you were giving her the part of Tina. Is that true?"

"I, uh, I . . . no. No, it isn't true, but you know . . ." I needed to plant the seed now. I needed to say something that would make Caitlin not want to play Tina. I'd been racking my brain all morning, but so far, nothing I thought of made much sense.

"I told Anysa and Karly that Hannah was making that up," Caitlin said. "I have more experience and I know the part much better than Hannah. Besides, if

I'm not going to be the lead, why in the world would I be in your club? And if I'm not in your club, my father is not going to help with the props."

"What did you say?" I asked.

This was the first I'd heard about this. Props?

"Yes, when I told Daddy that I was in your wonderful play he said he'd help us with the props. In fact, he said he could get us some professional props from the Broadwater Theater. One of his clients is an actor there. Didn't I tell you about this?"

Was this a setup? She hadn't told me about this and I'm sure she knew it. She just wanted to be certain that the part of Tina was hers and not Hannah's.

"You mean your Daddy can get us real props?" I said.

"Sure! He said we could use the theater company's costumes, too! Isn't that great?" she asked.

"No, I mean, yes, yes. I would love to have real costumes and props. Thanks!"

What was I saying? I didn't want to give the part to Caitlin just because her father could help us with props and costumes. I wanted to be fair to Hannah, too. But Caitlin was the best at reading the part. She had experience and she could help turn my play into a professional production. But what about Hannah? She wasn't even speaking to me.

I was starting to convince myself that Hannah wasn't the right person for the part. Then I remembered I'd almost promised the part of Tina to Hannah. I thought about my problem as I ate my lunch. I didn't even taste the mashed potatoes. I had almost finished eating when I saw Hannah was sitting all alone. I walked over to her.

"You speaking to me yet?"

"It wasn't me who stopped speaking," she said.

"Don't turn things around. I've been speaking."

"Hardly. Why did you leave your friends?" she asked. "Did you come over here to pick on me like the rest of your buddies?"

"I would never do that. I wanted to ask you something. I think I need someone to help me direct the play. There are more people involved than I thought. I was hoping you could help me direct instead of being in the play. It's just a stupid play, anyway. It's the directing experience that'll help us later, don't you think?"

I wasn't exactly being dishonest. I did feel a little overwhelmed. This play could be huge. We were going to have real props and real costumes and put it on in the auditorium. I needed a director to help me. Hannah knew the play and she was good at telling people what to do. She'd make a great director. I should have thought of this a long time ago.

I smiled. "What do you say?"

"Do I look stupid to you?" Hannah said angrily. "You want to give the part to Caitlin, don't you? Caitlin always gets her way! Caitlin Mullen, the Queen of the Fifth Grade! All she has to do is snap those fancy French polished fingers and you come running. Well, you know what? I don't want to be the director! When you used to be my best friend you said that I could have the leading lady part. And that's what I want to do."

"Best friend? Since when?" I said. It slipped out, honest. Just like that. I didn't mean it that way.

"Oh, wait," Hannah said. "You never said you

were my best friend. Sorry. But back when no one else wanted to eat with you, you told me that I could play Tina. Remember? I am not letting you off the hook. A deal's a deal."

I watched her gather her milk carton, place it on the tray, and walk away. I was trapped. Both Caitlin and Hannah wanted the lead part. I know I said that Hannah could have the lead. And now I had practically said it was Caitlin's. What was I going to do? My life was ruined. How could I be in this situation? My first big play, with real props and costumes, and here I was stuck between Caitlin and Hannah.

I had never been so popular. It seemed like everyone wanted a part of some kind in the play. A boy named Sonny even offered to be my codirector. I accepted mainly because I was in a daze. What was I going to do?

# Chapter Eleven

And the Leading Lady Is . . . ?

After I did my homework, I decided to talk to Momma. Her bedroom door was closed. I knocked softly.

"Momma, can I come in?"

"I'm not feeling too well, baby," Momma said. "In fact, I was hoping you and Sandra could order a pizza tonight. Make sure you save your Daddy some. He'll be home late tonight."

I couldn't remember the last time Momma was ill. I wondered if she had a cold. Maybe I could hug and kiss her and catch it. Then I wouldn't have to go to school tomorrow. After thinking about it for a minute, I decided that being sick wouldn't work. If I didn't face everyone tomorrow with my decision about the play, then I'd just have to do it the next day.

I walked past Sandra's room. I figured I must be desperate to even consider talking to Sandra. She couldn't help me. No one could. I guess desperation will make you do almost anything, so I knocked on her door. She pointed to a new sign on her wall:

NO ALIENS, NO PESTS,

AND NO PESKY ALIEN SISTERS.

I wanted to turn around and march back to my room. But I didn't. I knocked again.

"What is it?" she said.

"Momma said for us to order a pizza," I blurted.

"Even you can do that, can't you? You pick up the phone, dial the number, and order the pizza. Can't you handle that?"

"Sandra, can I talk to you for a minute?" I said.

Sandra sat up on the bed. She was blowing her nails dry with her tiny handheld dryer. I was about to suggest that she use her warm dragon breath to make her nails dry faster. But I needed her help, and insulting her wasn't the way to get it.

"Please," I said.

She turned the dryer off. "Please" between us was like a secret code. I almost never said it to her and she rarely said it to me — unless something was really, truly wrong.

"What's wrong?"

I sat down next to her on the bed.

"Don't sit on my bed! Your jeans are filthy! Sit over there on the chair."

I moved over to the chair.

"No smart remark? This must be serious. What's the matter?" she asked.

I explained the problem I was having with Caitlin, Hannah, and the play.

"You've got a huge problem," she said. "No matter what you do, someone's going to be mad at you."

I bit my lower lip, otherwise I'd say, "Tell me something I don't know."

"Okay," Sandra said. "You say that Caitlin Mullen is the best person for the part, right? And if she

101

doesn't get the part, you won't have any props or costumes."

"That's right," I said.

"Then there's Hannah, who you promised the part to."

"Not promised," I said. "I just told her she had the part."

"Whatever. The fact is you told her she had the part and now you don't want to give it to her. You're in big trouble."

This wasn't getting me anywhere. I already knew I had a huge problem. I stood up.

"You're not helping me much, but thanks anyway," I said.

"Wait a minute. Let me think for a second," Sandra said. "You just dumped this problem on me. I need a minute to think about it."

I sat back down. I heard my stomach growling. I should have ordered the pizza before I started this. I sighed heavily.

"Sandra," I said. "Do you mind if I order the pizza while you're thinking?"

"Go ahead," Sandra said. "I think better on a full stomach."

I started to say that she should eat all the time, but I kept quiet. I ordered a large pizza with everything on it except for jalapeños and anchovies. Yuck!

I sat back down and waited quietly for Sandra to figure things out. If anyone could get me out of this, it was Sandra.

I shifted uneasily in the chair. I wished she had a pillow on it. This chair was hard. No wonder she always sat on her bed.

"Sandra," I said, "are . . ."

"Yes, I'm thinking. But if you keep talking, I'm going to stop."

I motioned that I was zipping my mouth so she could think.

"I've got it," she said. "You can tell them that someone else is choosing the people for the parts."

"Someone like who, Sandra?" I asked.

"Make up somebody. That's it! Tell them that you hired a professional actor to choose each part. Hmm," she said. "Did you videotape their auditions?"

I frowned. "No, of course not! Sandra, that won't work. Keep thinking."

"I've got it." Sandra smiled. "Pick someone totally different for the part."

"Then they'll both be mad at me! Besides, Hannah's mom helped us get the auditorium, and Caitlin's dad is helping us get the props and costumes."

"Okay, you're right. How about . . ."

"Sandra, that's okay. I think I'll worry about it tomorrow," I said. "Thanks, anyway."

"Maybe I'll think of something after I eat," Sandra said.

"I sure hope so," I said. "I need all the help I can get."

At school the next day, things went from bad to worse. Everybody was talking about Hannah and Caitlin and about how both girls were saying that they had the part. Mr. Mullen came by the school. He told the principal that he had borrowed $1,000 worth of lighting equipment so Caitlin could perform in a proper setting. He congratulated me for founding the club. I tried to say that Hannah founded it with me, but no one wanted to listen.

Just before lunch, Ms. Bailes said, "Sharie, are you going to make us wait in suspense all day? Why don't you tell us who the leading lady is?"

I knew she meant well. I said, "I'd rather wait until after school."

Hannah excused herself to use the bathroom. I could see the tears in her eyes as she passed by my desk.

At lunch, Caitlin pulled me to the side, "Guess what."

"What?" I asked.

"My father says if you do a good job, he's going to recommend you for my theater summer school. You can't get in without a recommendation. I am so thrilled for you!"

"Thanks," I said. "Tell your daddy we'll see."

At lunch, Hannah waved at me from across the cafeteria. I couldn't talk to her, not now. I went to the library so I could think without having to talk to anyone.

*  *  *

After school, I thought about not showing up to announce my decision about the play. I had to make myself go down to the auditorium.

I stood on the stage and looked out at the crowd. Caitlin smiled and waved at me. I looked away. Hannah was sitting in the back of the auditorium by herself. Looking at her made me feel sad.

I pushed everything out of my mind and looked down at my list.

"When I call out your name, please come up and pick up a copy of the script. Inside your script, you will find out which part you're playing."

I called out the names. When I finished, I put my tablet on the table. Some people were stagehands, some were working on the lighting, some were extras, and others were arranging the props or doing the sound. Everyone's name had been called except Hannah Lowenstein and Caitlin Mullen.

Caitlin's friends ran over to her, whispering. They huddled in a circle, quickly flipping pages of the two scripts left that had no name on the outside. I felt bad. They wouldn't find a highlighted section.

Hannah stood alone, acting as though she were watching a tennis match. Her gaze went from me to Queen Caitlin and her court, to the bunch of other kids who were all excitedly asking me questions.

Now came the hard part. I'd spent all night trying to make a decision. I finally came up with a plan. It was the only thing I could think to do. I cleared my throat.

"Listen up, everybody," I said.

Only Hannah looked in my direction.

"Be quiet!" I said.

Silence filled the room. You could hear a pin drop. "Listen, you all know that Caitlin and Hannah both tried out for the part of Tina."

A few people nodded their heads. I could see Caitlin's friends whispering to each other.

Hannah watched me like she was in some kind of trance.

This wasn't going the way I imagined it would.

"I'm going to let both Hannah and Caitlin do the part together."

They both said, "What?"

At least I had them doing something in unison.

"I know what you're thinking," I said, "but . . ."

"You don't know what I'm thinking," Hannah said.

Caitlin said, "Well, you know what I'm thinking. I'm thinking this is going to be just another run-of-the-mill fifth-grade play using whatever you can find for props, costumes, and lights."

She folded her arms over her chest and glared at me. Anysa and Karly glared at me, too.

I stood for a minute looking at everyone staring or glaring at me. I walked out. I couldn't take it anymore. Either they would share the part or I'd get someone else. What else could I do?

# Chapter Twelve

## A Little Research Goes a Long Way

Later that night, blabbermouth Sandra helped me out. If helping means hanging you out to dry.

We were eating dinner when she said, "Sharie passed out parts for her play, Daddy."

"That's great, pumpkin."

Momma said, "Are you going to let Hannah dress herself?"

"I sure hope not," Daddy said. "I don't understand why her mother lets her dress like that."

"Hannah's not the lead," Sandra said. "At least not by herself."

"What does that mean?" Momma said. "I thought Hannah was playing the part of Tina."

"Tell them," Sandra said.

I glared at her. "You mean you want me to tell them about the P.S. on that letter?"

"No, no," Sandra said quickly. "Let's talk about something besides Sharie's play," Sandra said, like talking about my play hadn't been her idea. "All we do is talk about her stuff. What about me?"

Daddy said, "What's wrong with you, Sandra? You were the one who brought up the play."

"Yes, but now I want to talk about my piano recital. Mrs. Harmon says I am the best piano student she's ever had. She's trying to get me an audition at one of the colleges."

Just like that, Momma and Daddy were swooning over their precious Sandra. And for once I was glad. I didn't have to explain why I decided to have two leading ladies or explain anything else about the play. Thank goodness for the P.S. in Sandra's letter. Every time I brought it up, she got off my back. I was saved one more time.

I escaped to my room. I sat at my desk, staring at the script. How were Caitlin and Hannah both going to play the same part? My head hurt. I put the script away, did my homework, and went to bed. I fell asleep quickly.

The minute I walked into class the next day, Ms. Bailes pulled me outside and said she needed to talk to me.

"What is this I hear about Caitlin and Hannah both being the same character in your play?"

I explained my problem to Ms. Bailes.

"I think you're going to have to figure out a better solution than that," she said. "Ms. Riemer wants to see you in her office."

This was beginning to get too complicated.

"What did I do now?" I asked.

"I don't know," Ms. Bailes said. "She just said go to the principal's office and wait for her if she's not there."

Going to the principal's office wasn't new to me. Even in military schools, my mouth usually won me a free visit to the principal's office. But this time was different. I hadn't done anything. Or had I?

I sat on a bench outside of the principal's office. When she called me to come in, I felt like my breakfast was on its way back up.

"Sit down, Miss Johnson," Ms. Riemer said. "I want to talk with you."

"Yes, ma'am," I said.

"You are an outspoken little girl, aren't you?" she said. "I like that. I just wanted to let you know how proud I am of the way you're using your talents. I'm also looking forward to seeing my goddaughter, Caitlin, in your play. I've missed her other performances onstage."

Goddaughter? What was I going to do now? The principal just happened to be Caitlin's godmother. It seemed to me that Caitlin controlled the universe. Evidently, Ms. Riemer didn't know Caitlin was sharing the part with Hannah. Now was the time to tell her. Or should I just let her find out later? I decided that I had had enough trouble for one day. For once, I was in the principal's office and I wasn't really in trouble. I smiled and stood up to leave.

"Thanks for everything, Ms. Riemer," I said.

"You're welcome, Sharie," Ms. Riemer said. "I'm looking forward to seeing your play. Just make sure you have an adult supervisor at your rehearsals."

"I will," I said.

I left the office and went back to class. Hannah and Caitlin ignored me all day. During lunch, I went to the library. Momma was still feeling ill and she wouldn't be working this week. I didn't want to talk to anyone, anyway.

Something had been bothering me for weeks. The more problems I had, the more I realized I really didn't know anything about directing a play. Nothing. I had been in a play at a church. Two plays really, if you also counted the nativity scene I was in once. But I didn't know the first thing about directing a play.

I could barely pay attention in class. Why hadn't I thought of this before? Here I was worried about who was going to play the leading role in my play when I should have been focused on how I would direct it.

I didn't even know if my play was written correctly. I have never even seen a real play script! What was I thinking?

Sandra always researches everything before she does it. Now I can see why. I decided to postpone the practice after school. I went to the principal's office and asked Ms. Jane, the secretary, if she'd make the announcement for me.

"Sure, honey," Ms. Jane said. "We'll do that right away!"

After school, I asked Momma to drop me off at the public library.

"What do you mean, drop you off?" Momma said crossly. She still wasn't feeling very well.

"I mean, drop me off at the library and then come back and pick me up," I said.

"Yeah, Momma," Sandra said. "And while you're at it, why don't you buy her a car so she can drive home by herself?"

"Just stay out of my business, Sandra," I said.

"Be quiet, you two!" Momma said. "I don't know what's gotten into you, Sharie. You're only ten! You're not old enough to be dropped off at a public library. We'll all go in. I want to look around, anyway."

I didn't want them to go in. I didn't want them seeing me getting books about playwriting and directing. Sandra would start picking on me about not knowing what I was doing. Momma would know I'd agreed to do something I didn't know anything about. And the worst thing about it, she would know I waited until now to look it up. The one thing she always said was to be prepared. I hated to admit it, but I wasn't prepared and I needed help. I decided that honesty was the best policy. Lying only got me into trouble.

"What books are you looking for?" Momma asked.

"I need to get some books on plays and directing," I said.

"Well, Sharie," Momma said. "I'm glad to see that you're finally getting what I've been trying to tell you all along."

"What do you mean, Momma?"

"That you need to admit when you don't know something . . . then find it out." She smiled.

Sometimes I had to admit, my momma was cool.

I got on the computer and wrote down the Dewey decimal numbers for the books I wanted. I was glad Momma made us learn about the Dewey decimal system when we got our first library cards. She always told us that whatever you need to know could probably be found in a library.

I checked out my books and we headed home. Sandra checked out some mysteries. Momma had a stack of books, but she carefully covered the titles so I couldn't see what she was reading. I wondered what all the mystery was about, but I was too worried about my play to ask any questions.

As soon as I finished my homework, I sat down at my desk to pore over the books. Right away I learned two things: I should have researched everything first and I couldn't do everything by myself.

I made a list of all the help I needed: a stage manager, a set designer, a sound person, a makeup artist, and a costume person. I'd given out things for people to do, but now I could see the assignments I had passed out had nothing to do with a play. I made a list of the qualities that each person would need accord-ing to the book.

"A stage manager needs to be organized, reliable, efficient, diplomatic, and assertive, without being bossy." Okay, that would automatically rule me out. Hmmm. Who did I know who fit this description? The only person I knew well was Hannah, and she wasn't even speaking to me.

I spent the rest of the night trying to figure out how to get the best people to help me. Then I thought, Wait, why am I acting like this is a big deal? Face it, I'm ten years old and this is a fifth-grade play. No-body's going to see it but the people at school and their families. What's the big deal? I started to relax.

The minute I got to school, Ms. Riemer asked me to come to her office. I wondered if I was in trouble. I couldn't remember shooting off my mouth lately.

"Come on in, Miss Johnson," she said, smiling like we were old friends. "Have a seat."

I sat down. I wondered what Ms. Riemer wanted now.

"Miss Johnson, I have some wonderful news for you," Ms. Riemer said. "Caitlin's father made arrangements for our play to be taped and then shown to all the schools in the district. Isn't that great?"

I swallowed hard. No, no it wasn't great. I had no idea what I was doing. And on top of that, Caitlin's dad would probably take away everything he'd offered us once he found out the truth. Caitlin was acting like she was the only lead. I had heard the kids teasing Hannah about it just this morning. This was a mess, a real ugly mess. Now everyone all over the city was going to see the play.

"Ms. Riemer, I don't know if it's a good idea to tape the play. I mean, this is my first play. Why don't we just present it here at Casey?"

"You don't understand," Ms. Riemer said. "We've been pushing our district for more arts programs. When they see a little ten-year-old girl take it upon herself to start an acting club and then produce a play, everyone will be impressed, especially the school board. Before you got involved with this play-acting club, your grades were slipping, your teacher was always after you to stop talking in class, and you always had something smart to say. Thanks to this play, you've turned yourself around, and all because you found an interest in the arts. Your play is just what we need to prove the value of the arts in school."

That's when it hit me. I had taken all the credit and Hannah had not made one complaint. She had not run around accusing me of stealing her idea. But in a way, I had. I had to make this right.

"Ms. Riemer, actually it was just as much Hannah Lowenstein's idea as it was mine," I said.

"Never mind all that. What we have to do is get some publicity. With Caitlin as the lead, I think I can talk her dad into working with us on placing stories in the newspaper and on the radio. Your play is a winner. It will help the school, the community, and it has already helped you, Miss Johnson. Good job! Now, get back to class."

I didn't know what to say. I tried to smile, but I couldn't. Everything was wrong, wrong, wrong, and it was all my fault. If I'd done my research and checked out those books about playwriting first, this wouldn't be happening. I would have known that I couldn't direct the play all alone. I would have realized that you can't have two people playing the same part unless one of them is the understudy. And more important, I would have made sure everyone knew this wasn't just my idea. I didn't know what to do.

# Chapter Thirteen

With Friends Like These,
Who Needs Enemies?

We had a rehearsal after school. When I saw everyone running around, I knew why a stage manager is so important. I was giving directions, but people kept bumping into one another. The worst part was that Caitlin and Hannah were both trying to be in the same place. When I called for Tina's character to come onstage, Hannah and Caitlin both ran up at the same time. They collided and landed in a heap on the floor. I forgot to say which Tina I wanted onstage.

As they scrambled to get up, Hannah stepped on Caitlin's skirt and tore it.

"You did that on purpose," she shouted at Hannah.

Hannah shouted back, "I did not."

"This is my most expensive skirt. My mom sent it to me from Paris," Caitlin cried. "You just want everyone to, to . . ." She was crying.

"I want everybody to what?" Hannah said.

"To wear raggedy clothes like you do," Caitlin shouted.

"What's going on here? Who told you kids you could be in here without a chaperone?"

I turned around to face the vice principal, Mr. Applegate. He looked really mad. "Whose idea was this?"

Everyone pointed at me.

"Come with me. Everyone else go home, right now."

I followed behind him. I had been so worried about everything else that I'd forgotten we were supposed to have an adult advisor at all of our meetings and practices. How could I have forgotten to ask someone to be our advisor? This was getting way out of hand. Mr. Applegate told me that I shouldn't have held the practice without permission. For once, I didn't say a word. I sat quietly, staring into space, wondering how I'd let things get so far out of hand.

I dragged myself home, hoping Mr. Applegate wouldn't call my parents. I didn't speak during dinner. I didn't want to eat, so I just pushed my food around on my plate.

Momma said, "What's the matter?"

"Nothing," I said.

After dinner, Sandra knocked on my door.

"What do you want?"

"Can I come in?" Sandra asked.

"Sure."

"What happened in here? Momma will kill you if she sees your room like this."

I looked around. I'd been so busy that I hadn't cleaned up in a week. I watched Sandra pick up one of my sweatshirts and fold it.

"Listen," she said, "I know you sort of got yourself in a mess. It seems like you're between a rock and a hard place, like Momma says sometimes. I respect that you didn't make a choice between your friends. I know we don't always get along, but as your big sister, I just want you to know that I hope you work this one out."

And just like that, she was gone. I pinched my arm. Was that Sandra or did an alien abduct my sister? She was right. I was between a rock and a hard place. How did I think I could manage two people in one part? I repeated it, two people with one part. That was it. Why didn't I think of this before? There was nothing that said that I couldn't have two leading ladies. I could have two leading parts and make them both equally important. I was the playwright. My job was to make the play work.

After reading the books, I'd come to understand that a play is never really finished. You could change it every single night, if you needed to, in order to make it work. That was it. I snatched up some paper and wrote quickly. I would create another part.

Tina could have a twin. They would be born on the same day but look completely different. I knew some twins like that when I lived in Kansas. They were called fraternal twins. I decided to call Tina's twin Tracey. Even though they have different person-alities, at the end of the play, you find out they're both very much alike.

I did it! I found a new theme for the play.

Tina is popular and Tracey is the outsider. Every-thing changes when they both run into a family prob-lem that can only be solved when they work together. That's when they both realize that even though they're totally different, there is one thing that makes them both the same — the love they have for each other as sisters.

I read it over. Wow. Did I just write that? I couldn't believe it. I worked on my play until Momma tapped on the door and said it was bedtime. I jumped up and ran out into the hall.

"I want to kiss you now, Momma," I said, pecking her on the cheek.

I didn't want her to come into my room.

"Where's Daddy? While I'm passing out kisses, I'll give him his bedtime kiss, too."

"Here I am," Daddy said.

I kissed him quickly and ran back into my room.

There was no way I would escape being grounded if Daddy saw my messy room. I scooped the clothes off of my bed and snuggled underneath the covers. For the first time in a long time, I had a peaceful night's rest.

The next morning, first thing, I talked to Ms. Bailes about being our drama club advisor. After reading the playwriting books, I realized there was no such thing as an acting club.

Next, I told Hannah about the new part I'd written for her. At first, she didn't say anything, so I just put the play on her desk. I practically held my breath waiting for her reaction. I kept turning around to see if she liked it. Hannah put the pages down and smiled at me. She gave me the thumbs-up.

Now all I had to do was convince Queen Caitlin that Hannah's role wouldn't take away from her part. She sat quietly and listened as I explained the new roles to her during our library time.

"I suppose that's okay," she said. She turned her head away from me, but I could see that she was crying.

"You'll still have just as much time onstage," I added.

"It's not that," Caitlin said. "I'm just afraid that if I don't have the leading role in the play, my momma won't fly here from Paris to see it. She's an actress, you know."

I didn't know that. It made me look at Caitlin a different way.

"My mother and father are separated. My mother decided that I'd be better off with my father since she travels so much. She always has the leading roles in her plays. Did I tell you that?"

I shook my head. I didn't know what to say.

"I miss my mother," Caitlin said sadly. "I haven't seen her in seven months. I thought she would come for my birthday, but she didn't. That's why my daddy tried to get Little James to perform for my birthday. The funny thing is, I really didn't want anyone but my mother there."

Annette's parents were separated, too. We used to talk about it all the time. Sometimes she spent the summer with her dad, and other times she spent holidays with her mom.

I couldn't imagine my life without both my parents. I wondered if I could survive being without my momma for seven months. I felt sorry for Caitlin. It just goes to show you that money and popularity aren't everything. I realized that this was the theme of my play. Here I was watching poor Hannah, thinking she was the outsider, when in reality Hannah and Caitlin are the same. They are both human beings, capable of being hurt.

"Hey, listen," I said. "Do you mind if I use a little of your life in the story? You don't have to tell your momma that there's another leading lady. According to a book I read, everyone is a lead in a play. Every part must be important to the story."

"Okay. Sure," she said, wiping her eyes. "My mother has never had a play based on her life."

"Good. Now I've just got to find a stage manager."

"I know someone," she said.

"Who?"

"Anysa. She's an excellent musician. Maybe you could use her. You need a person in charge of sound, right?"

"Yes, sure. But that's called a sound designer.

That's different from a stage manager. I need to find someone who's nice to everyone and not bossy, but can keep order backstage. You know, someone totally different from you."

I rolled my eyes. Me and my big mouth!

"I didn't mean . . ."

"That's okay," Caitlin said. "You're bossy, too."

She was right. We smiled at each other.

"I'll see you at practice," I said.

"I'll be there," Caitlin said.

I spent my lunch hour reassigning people to the positions I read about in my books. Now I had a makeup artist, a prop manager, and a sound designer, but I still didn't have a stage manager. I had assigned a job to almost everyone in the fifth grade.

Ms. Bailes called to me as I was on my way to the auditorium.

"Sharie, wait a minute. I need to talk to you about something. I need you to do me a favor."

"No problem. What is it?" I asked her, thinking what a cool teacher she was.

"I heard you were looking for a stage manager. Would you mind asking Woody Lane?"

I stared at her. Was she serious? Woody Lane?

"I don't think he could do it, Ms. Bailes. I mean, Woody Lane is a, well, I hate to say it, but he's a dork."

"A dork?" she said.

"You know, he just sits and stares off into space. I don't think I've ever heard him say a word. The stage manager is an important job. I mean, he has to be reliable, dependable, and able to keep up with a bunch of things at once."

"Woody can do that," Ms. Bailes said.

"But the stage manager has to be diplomatic. You know, get people to do what he wants without being bossy. In other words, the kids need to want to do what he tells them to do. I don't think . . ."

"Would you at least try him out?" Ms. Bailes said. "For me?"

I didn't have time to take a chance on Woody. I needed someone who was going to take charge. I looked at Ms. Bailes. I wanted to tell her no, but she had always been so nice to me. I didn't want to disappoint her.

"Okay, Ms. Bailes. I'll try him out. Tell him to come to the meeting tomorrow."

"I've already invited him, just in case you said yes. He doesn't know I'm asking you, so if you don't mind, just tell him you thought of him."

I shrugged. "Okay, Ms. Bailes."

"Great," she said, smiling.

At dinner, I told Momma and Daddy how things were working out. Momma said she was glad I finally learned to do research and read before starting a project. Daddy said he was proud that I found a way to be loyal to both my friends.

When we finished dinner, Daddy said we needed to have a family meeting. He said they had a big announcement to make.

The last meeting we'd had was about us not keeping our rooms neat enough. I moaned. Why didn't I clean my room? I knew this was going to happen.

"Sandra," I whispered. "Is your room messy, too?"

"No," Sandra whispered back. "And I cleaned yours up while you were downstairs helping Momma fix dinner."

"You did?" I said. I couldn't believe it. "Thanks!"

"That's okay. Thanks for giving me back my letter."

I'd secretly given Sandra back her letter the other day. I wanted to do something nice for her since she had tried to help me.

"Well, then, what are we in trouble for?" I whispered.

"I don't know," Sandra said. "Maybe they have good news for us."

# Chapter Fourteen

## The Big Announcement

We sat in our usual spots on the couch and waited. Daddy always drew everything out. Momma sat in the stuffed side chair. Daddy sat on the arm of the chair. They kept smiling at each other.

I wondered if we were moving again and Momma was just pretending to be happy. I sighed. I would not move. Nope. This time I would stand my ground. I liked this school. Ms. Bailes was one of the best teachers I'd ever had. And now I was doing something fun. I was directing a fifth-grade play that was going to help the community. Ms. Riemer herself said so. I would not go.

Daddy cleared his throat. Sandra and I made our usual family meeting eye contact, which meant, Oh, no.

"Girls, you know that your momma hasn't been feeling well lately," he began.

I stared at Sandra, confused. If Momma was sick, why were they trying so hard to stop giggling?

"Well, there's no easy way to say this, but we're going to have another person in the house," Daddy said. Then both Momma and Daddy burst into giggles.

I frowned. "What other person?" The last time we had another person it was Uncle Johnny, Daddy's oldest brother. He didn't do anything but watch television and burp loudly. Daddy finally had to ask him to leave.

"I hope it's not Uncle Burpy," I said.

Oops, I didn't mean to say that.

"No, it's not your Uncle Johnny!" Daddy said. He was actually laughing.

Sandra said, "So who's moving in?"

"And what does Momma not feeling well have to

do with it?" I asked. "Wait. I've got it. Sandra, our dreams have come true!"

"So," Daddy said. "You already know?"

"Sure," I said. Now it all made sense. "Momma's not feeling well, so she can't clean up or cook as much. Now everything makes sense!"

"That's right," Daddy said. "See, I told you, honey. I knew our girls would be happy."

"We're going to get a live-in maid, aren't we?" I said happily. "Momma's too sick to clean. Daddy's too busy. We don't do a very good job sometimes, so we need a live-in maid! Yeah!"

Momma was taking a sip of tea. She started to cough.

"When is she going to start working for us? I've been too busy to clean my room lately."

Sandra pinched me. "Be quiet, silly. We're not getting a maid."

"Well, who's coming to live with us? If it's not a maid, and it's not one of our relatives . . ."

"Who said it wasn't a relative?" Daddy said.

"Who is it? We don't have any other relatives who would want to come and live with us, do we?"

"Not yet," Momma said, rubbing her stomach like Santa Claus does.

I didn't get it. Now all three of them were giggling. "Okay, I give up. Who is it?"

"Momma's going to have a baby," Sandra said.

"A baby?" I said. "A baby!"

"Yes, we're going to have a baby sister or a brother," Sandra said. "Do you know whether it's a girl or a boy yet, Momma?"

"It's a girl," Momma said. She started giggling.

I was speechless. I didn't want a baby sister. I was just starting to get along with the one sister I had. Now I'd be sandwiched in the middle between two sisters. I'd have an older sister who wouldn't pay any attention to me and a younger sister everyone would be paying attention to. I'd rather have a dog.

"Okay, I'm going to bed," I said.

"Wait a minute," Momma said. "Is that all you're going to say?"

"Don't be so selfish, Sharie," Daddy said. "Tell your momma that you're happy for us."

"Are you upset, baby?" Momma said.

"Don't call me baby, Momma," I said. "I keep telling you I'm not a baby!"

"See, I told you she'd be upset, Howard," Momma said.

Of course I was upset. What did they expect? Sandra wasn't upset because she was still going to be the oldest. But now, I wouldn't be anything except the one in the middle. On top of that, I'd have a bossy older sister to deal with and a pesky baby sister. It was too much to handle.

"I'm tired," I said. "Good night. I'm going to bed."

"Good night, Bab — Sharie," Momma said. "That's okay, Howard," I heard Momma say as I left the room. "She just needs time to get used to the idea. Don't worry."

I got into bed and stared at the ceiling for a long time, thinking about the new baby. Then it hit me! I might be in the middle, but I wouldn't be the baby anymore. I wouldn't be the oldest, but I'd be the big sister to the baby! The baby would have to do what I said because I'm older. Maybe this baby thing wouldn't be so bad after all. I felt better for the first time all evening. I drifted off to sleep dreaming about babies.

# Chapter Fifteen

## Showtime!

When I got to school, I was surprised to see signs up about our practice after school. Who put them up? I assumed it was Ms. Bailes and I thanked her for putting the signs up. I had forgotten about doing them.

"I didn't put them up," Ms. Bailes said.

"Then who did?" I asked. She pointed to Woody Lane. He was sitting in a corner busily making more signs.

I walked over to him. "Thanks for putting the signs up."

"You're welcome," he said firmly.

I don't know why, but I expected his voice to be a skinny, wimpy little voice, not a strong voice.

"Here," he said, pushing a clipboard toward me. "I've made a list of all the things you'll need. I've also put it on the school computer so it's easy for you to change. I've set it up so that if you make a change in the script that affects the props, the list will change automatically."

Woody handed me another stack of papers.

"Here's the schedule of all our practices, the number of practices you need to schedule, and a list of all the props and costumes."

I was speechless when he finished. I found out later that Woody had straight A's and that he'd never been late for class. Wow. He was the perfect stage manager. I couldn't believe that someone who looked so out of it could be so organized.

I worked on the play every night. I felt a little better about directing, but my two leading ladies were driving me nuts. For the last three days, all I'd done was try to make them both happy.

Hannah felt like her lines weren't right for her character. She rewrote some of her part. At first, I was upset, but then I realized Hannah was right. I added the new lines to the play and erased the ones I'd written.

Queen Caitlin wanted more lines. She told me that she wanted Hannah's part changed so that her mother would think she had the lead role all to herself.

"You can't have the lead role to yourself," I told Caitlin. "We've been through this before. You and Hannah both have equal parts. Woody even counted the lines. Okay?"

"No, it's not okay. I told you that it's very important that I have the lead role," Caitlin said.

Now I was boiling mad.

"If you don't want the part, I'll just have to find someone else," I said.

"You can't give my role to anyone else," Caitlin said. "This is a school play. What makes you think you're the boss, anyway?"

I took out one of my playwriting books; I opened to the page on directors.

"According to this, I am the boss," I said. "Let's go in the hallway and talk about this."

"Well, come on, then," Caitlin said. She walked off the stage and stormed out of the auditorium.

I felt sick. Just as I was beginning to like her, she pulls a trick like this. Everyone was staring at me. I took a deep breath. I was the director, so I did the only thing I could do, I directed.

"Could someone read Caitlin's part while we're gone?" I said as if nothing had happened.

"I can do both parts," Hannah said. "Don't worry."

"Thanks," I said.

Hannah gave me a thumbs-up and smiled at me. I started to feel better.

"Okay, everyone," I said. "Hannah will read Caitlin's part. Take your places, please, and start from act one. I'll be right back."

"Do you want me to come outside and talk with Caitlin, too?" Ms. Bailes asked. "That's my job as the drama club advisor, you know — to advise."

"No, thank you," I said. "Let me talk to Caitlin first. If I can't work things out, I'll let you know."

"Okay," Ms. Bailes said. "I'll take care of everything while you're gone."

"Thanks," I said as I pushed open the door that led to the hallway.

Caitlin was sitting on a bench near the door. She was twirling her hair around her finger. I noticed she does that when she's nervous or upset. I took a deep breath and tried to think of something to say.

"Okay, Caitlin," I said. "I'm your friend, so tell me what's wrong. I know something is bothering you besides the play."

"I'm okay," Caitlin said stiffly.

"No, you're not," I said. "You're twirling your hair. You always do that when you're upset."

Caitlin stopped twisting her hair and stared at me.

"Caitlin, you're one of the leading ladies and you need to start acting like it," I said. "Everyone looks up to you. You open the play and you close the play. You have the same number of lines as Hannah. We've been over this before and I know you understand that. So what's really bothering you?"

"I don't know if my mother's coming to the play," Caitlin said as tears slowly slid down her face. "I thought if I told her how important my part is that she'd try harder to come."

Caitlin reached inside her sleeve and pulled out her handkerchief. She wiped her eyes.

"I guess that's a good place for a hanky after all," I said.

"I feel m-e-l-a-n-c-h-o-l-y," Caitlin said.

"I'm sorry," I said. "Look, maybe you need to tell your mother how much you need to see her and quit worrying about your part in the play. Have you ever told her how much you miss her?"

"Not really," Caitlin said. "I try to pretend everything is fine so she won't be upset."

"But everything isn't fine. You're upset," I said. "Maybe you need to tell her that."

Caitlin sat quietly for a minute. She reached up to grab a lock of hair. I gently moved her hand away. She smiled at me.

"Thanks," Caitlin said.

"That's what friends are for," I said.

"Come on!" Caitlin said. "We've got a play to put on!"

I smiled at her and we went back inside. It felt good to help Caitlin. I've gone from being alone at Casey to making two good friends in just a few months. Things were finally getting better at school.

After dinner, Momma went to bed. She was sick all the time, morning, noon, and night. She spent most of her days in bed.

"I thought it was called morning sickness because you only felt bad in the morning," I said.

"Well, Momma feels bad all the time," Sandra said. "Come on, let's clean the kitchen."

I helped Sandra clear the table and wash the dishes. Sandra was looking forward to the new baby. When Momma felt well enough, she and Sandra went shopping for things for the baby. I didn't go. I didn't want to look at baby things. It was too boring. All Momma and Sandra said while they shopped was "Oooh, how cute!" or "Ahhh, that's darling." Yuck!

Since they found out about the baby, Momma and Daddy didn't stay on my case about everything so much. They were busy with doctor's appointments and buying baby clothes and furniture. They also started to give me a little more freedom, just like Sandra. It was nice to know that they felt I was growing up and could be a little more responsible.

I tried to keep my room clean, do my homework, and take care of my chores without them having to tell me over and over again. Maybe that was Sandra's secret. She acted like a grown-up, so they treated her like one.

The play was only a few days away, but rehearsals were going pretty well. Hannah and Caitlin were friendly to me again, but they still didn't hang out with each other. I knew that even though they worked together on the play, they still didn't like each other. Hannah could be overbearing, too, just like Caitlin. Maybe that came with the leading lady role. They acted like this play was going to be on Broadway instead of in the Casey Elementary School auditorium.

Caitlin's dad arranged for Hannah, Caitlin, and me to be interviewed by the local newspaper. I was nervous and sweaty. We sat in the principal's office waiting for the reporter and the cameraperson to arrive. None of us were talking or looking at each other.

During the interview, Caitlin took credit for the idea of getting two totally opposite people to play the lead roles. She also insisted that she was the only "leading lady."

The reporter nodded every time Caitlin said a word. The next morning, when I read the article, I understood why. The reporter's last name was Mullen, too. It turns out that she is Caitlin's cousin. I apologized to Hannah for not explaining everything to the reporter.

"Oh, I understand," Hannah said. "You've got her dad giving you the props, the lights, and the costumes. And her dad's arranging the publicity. What can you do?"

"Nothing, I guess," I said.

"I forgive you," Hannah said. "Do you want to be best friends again?"

This time I didn't hesitate. "Yes, best friends." Annette would understand, I was sure. We hugged.

"I've missed you," I said.

"I've missed you, too," Hannah said.

Finally, it was the night of the play. Caitlin's mother showed up just before the play started. Caitlin was almost in tears because she didn't think she was coming.

When her mother finally arrived, everyone started to whisper and point at her. She had three people following her around — taking her coat, holding her things, and taking her picture. People came up to her to ask for her autograph. She waved when she saw Caitlin peeking out from behind the curtain. Caitlin waved back. I pulled her away from the curtain so we could get started. It was almost showtime. I told everyone how much I appreciated their hard work and their suggestions. I thanked Ms. Bailes for her help. Caitlin and Hannah gave me a hug. They did it at the same time, so they accidentally hugged each other, too. I hoped that after the play was over we could all be friends. Juggling Caitlin and Hannah was wearing me out.

"It's time to start," Ms. Bailes said.

"Okay, everyone," I said. "Take your places."

Then Woody dimmed the lights and the play began. I was almost too nervous to watch! But it actually went okay. There were a few mistakes here and there, but no big ones. When it was over, everyone came out and took a bow.

Caitlin and Hannah held hands and bowed together. That made me happy. Then Woody pushed me forward and I got a standing ovation! I couldn't believe it. Afterward, people kept saying that they were stunned that a ten year old wrote such a professional play!

Ms. Bailes introduced me to one of her friends, Mr. Williams, who was a real playwright and director. He told me that he thought that I did a good job.

"She's our bab — our big girl," Daddy said. He gave me a big hug.

"How old are you?" Mr. Williams asked.

"She's ten," Momma said.

"Well, you're not a baby, anymore. Next summer, you can sign up for our Young Actors Workshop. It's

a summer drama camp in San Antonio. Are you interested?"

"Yes, yes, I'm interested. Can I go, Daddy, please can I go?" I begged.

Momma said, "I don't think so, Sharie. You're not old enough to go away from home by yourself."

"Sandra can go with me," I pleaded.

"Don't look at me," Sandra said. "I'm off to music camp next summer. Besides, Momma, I went to my first music camp when I was ten. I don't see why Sharie can't go by herself."

"That's right," Ms. Bailes said. "It took a pretty grown-up and mature young lady to pull this play off. Are you sure she can't go? They have close supervision at all times. And they're busy day and night preparing their plays. I work as a camp supervisor there every summer. I can keep an eye on her."

"Momma, please let me go," I begged. "I'm not the baby, anymore."

I watched Momma whispering to Daddy. I crossed my fingers. I anxiously waited for them to say something.

"Please," I said. "I'm not a baby."

"Okay, you can go," Momma finally said. "But only if you keep up your grades for the entire year."

"Yes," Daddy said, "I think you've earned our trust. You're growing up. But don't forget, you'll always be our baby."

Just then, I understood a very important thing. I would always be their baby because they loved me.

I smiled. "Sure, Daddy and Momma. I know. I'll always be your baby."

I couldn't wait until this new baby girl joined the family. Maybe, just maybe, it would take some of the heat off me. Surely she couldn't be as perfect as Miss Sandra. Yes, a new baby was just what this family needed. I hugged Momma and Daddy. Sandra squeezed in next to me. I gave her a big hug, too.

"P.S.," I said to Sandra. "I love you, too."